SIXKILL

SIXKILL

ROBERT B. PARKER

Quercus

First published in Great Britain in 2011 by

Quercus
21 Bloomsbury Square
London
WC1A 2NS

A CIP catalogue record for this book is available
from the British Library

ISBN (HB) 978 0 85738 211 5
ISBN (TPB) 978 0 85738 212 2

Printed and bound in Great Britain by Clays Ltd, St Ives plc

10 9 8 7 6 5 4 3 2 1

As always, for Joan.

And this one's for Lou Zambello.

SIXKILL

IT WAS SPRING. The vernal equinox had done whatever it was it did, and the late March air drifting in through the open window in my office was soft even though it wasn't really warm yet. Spring training was under way in full tiresomeness, and opening day was two weeks off.

I was drinking coffee and studying a new comic strip called *Frazz* to see if there were any existential implications that I might be missing, when Quirk came in and went to the coffeepot, poured himself a cup, added sugar and condensed milk, and took a seat opposite my desk.

"Care for coffee?" I said.

"Got some," Quirk said. "Nice of you to ask."

"You ever read *Frazz*?" I said.

"What the fuck is *Frazz*," Quirk said.

He was as big as I was, which is biggish, and always dressed well. Today he had on a chestnut-colored Harris tweed jacket. His hands were thick, and there was in his eyes a look of implacable resolution that made most people careful with him.

"A comic strip in the *Globe*," I said. "It's new."

"I'm a grown man," Quirk said.

"And a police captain," I said.

"Exactly," Quirk said. "I don't read comic strips."

"I withdraw the question," I said.

Quirk nodded.

"I need something," he said.

"Everyone says so."

He ignored me. Quirk ignored a lot. He wasn't being impolite. He was merely focused, and I had known for years that he cared very little what other people thought.

"You know about Jumbo Nelson?"

"The actor," I said.

"Yes."

"Here shooting a movie," I said.

"Yeah."

"You guys think he murdered a young woman," I said.

"He's a person of interest," Quirk said.

I looked at him. I'd known him a long time.

"And?" I said.

"Lemme fill you in," Quirk said.

I got up and poured myself more coffee, and warmed Quirk's

up. Then I put the pot on the burner, sat down in my chair, and leaned back with my feet up.

"Do," I said.

"Real name's Jeremy Franklin Nelson," Quirk said. "Ever seen him?"

"Seen his photograph," I said. "Never seen a movie."

"Photo's enough," Quirk said. "You can see where the nickname came from."

"I can," I said.

"He's in town," Quirk said, "shooting a movie. Which you know."

"As yet untitled," I said.

"*Frazz* tell you that?" Quirk said.

"I'm adventurous," I said. "Sometimes I read other stuff."

"Fucking media's treating this like it was the Lindbergh kidnapping."

"Lotta media to fill," I said.

"Too much," Quirk said. "Always was. Anyway, Jumbo is in town, travels with a bodyguard, an Indian."

"A Native American?"

Quirk nodded.

"Like I said."

"Could be an India Indian," I said.

"This guy's American Indian," Quirk said. "Wait'll you get a load of him."

"Dangerous?" I said.

"I dunno," Quirk said. "Looks good."

"Bodyguard involved?" I said.

"In the crime? Not that I know of," Quirk said.

"Press tells me that Jumbo raped and murdered a young woman and should be beheaded at once."

"Yeah," Quirk said. "That's what they tell me, too. What everybody tells me."

"You have doubts?"

Quirk shrugged.

"Here's what I know," he said. "Girl's name is Dawn Lopata, twenty years old, graduated last year from Bunker Hill Community College, was not employed."

Quirk sipped some coffee.

"More sugar," he said.

He went to the coffeemaker on the file cabinet and got some, and stirred it in, and sat back down. He took another sip and nodded.

"She's watching them shoot a scene outdoors on the Common, near Park Street Station, and Jumbo spots her. He sends a production assistant over to invite her to have lunch with him in the commissary. She's thrilled."

"As I would be," I said.

"Yeah," Quirk said. "Me too. So she has lunch with all the stars and the movie crew, and Jumbo gets her phone number and says maybe they can get together later, and she says oh-wow-yes."

"Do you know she said that?"

"The oh-wow-yes?" Quirk said. "No. So he calls her that night and she goes over to his hotel. They drink some champagne. They do some lines. They have sex. When they get through, they get dressed. Jumbo excuses himself for a moment while he goes to the bathroom. And while he's gone she lies back down on the bed and dies."

"I was having sex with Jumbo Nelson," I said, "I might consider it myself."

"It was after," Quirk said.

"Maybe she died of shame," I said.

"There was considerable bruising around the vaginal area," Quirk said.

"Suggesting an, ah, accessory object?"

"ME isn't sure," Quirk said. "Maybe Jumbo really is jumbo."

"Cause of death?" I said.

"ME thinks it's asphyxiation," Quirk said. "They found some ligature marks on her neck. But they don't seem entirely comfortable with how they got there."

"They're not sure?" I said.

"No."

"Aren't they supposed to be sure?" I said.

"For crissake," Quirk said. "One case I had, they lost the fucking body."

"That would be disheartening," I said.

"Was," Quirk said. "Also, when they're not sure, it gives a lot of space for rumors."

"I heard one report that the accessory object was the neck of a champagne bottle and it broke inside her and she bled to death."

Quirk shook his head.

"I know," Quirk said. "No evidence of it."

"I don't think the Internet requires evidence."

"Or knows how to get it," Quirk said.

"How 'bout Jumbo?" I said.

"Says he doesn't know what happened. Admits he was whacked on coke and booze. He says he left her alone and when he came back in the bedroom, he notices she's not responsive. Tries to wake her up. Can't. And calls nine-one-one."

"He'd been on top of her?" I said.

"Apparently," Quirk said. "At some point."

"Jesus," I said.

"I know, and we've thought about that."

"How much does he weigh?" I said.

"Don't know," Quirk said. "I'd say three-fifty to four hundred. He claims he doesn't know, either."

"What kind of guy is he?" I said.

"Awful," Quirk said. "Food, booze, dope, sex. Never saw a girl too young. Or a guy."

"Long as it's alive?" I said.

"I don't know if he requires that," Quirk said.

"But a nice guy aside from his hobbies," I said.

"Loud, arrogant, stupid, foulmouthed," Quirk said.

"*You* think he's foulmouthed?"

"Fucking A," Quirk said.

SPRING WAS STILL drifting in.

"Everybody likes him for it," Quirk said. "Us, the studio, people on the crew, everybody. Girl's parents."

"You like him for it?" I said.

"Governor likes him for it. Mayor likes him for it. Commissioner loves him. Command staff loves him more. Senate president. House speaker. Both newspapers. Everybody on TV. Every fucking cyberspace moron who can type," Quirk said.

"You?" I said.

"I don't think he murdered her," Quirk said. "Or if he did, we don't have enough hard evidence to say it. We're guessing."

"And everybody wants it to go away and take him with it," I said.

"They do," Quirk said. "He was probably with her when she died, and what they were doing may have killed her, I don't know. But I don't think you can convict a guy of murder on what we've got, and I'm afraid we might."

"The fact that he's a creep helps move it along," I said.

"It's not illegal to be a pain in the ass," Quirk said. "It was, you and me probably be doing time."

"Maybe you," I said. "Whaddya need from me?"

"I want you to look into it," Quirk said.

"Because you can't?"

"Correct," Quirk said.

"Anybody gonna pay me?" I said.

"The movie studio has hired Rita Fiore to represent Jumbo," Quirk said. "I've talked to her. She says Cone, Oakes will hire you to investigate."

"And bill the studio," I said.

"Be my guess," Quirk said.

"What makes you think he didn't commit first-degree murder?" I said.

"Maybe he did," Quirk said. "And if he did, we'll try to prove it. But right now I think he's being railroaded, and I can't stop it and stay a cop."

"What if I find out that he's guilty as charged?"

"Tell me," Quirk said. "I'll be thrilled. You want to look at our notes, so far?"

"I like to start fresh," I said. "I think better if I'm in the process."

"Yeah," Quirk said. "I know."

"Okay," I said.

"Okay you'll take the job?"

"Yep."

"Just like that?" Quirk said.

"Yep," I said.

"You might start out by talking to Rita Fiore," Quirk said.

"You might start out by not telling me what to do," I said.

"Okay," Quirk said. "What are you gonna do?"

"I'm gonna talk to Rita Fiore," I said.

"Good idea," Quirk said.

He almost smiled.

PEARL SCRATCHED at the bedroom door.

Susan got out of bed naked and let Pearl in, then came back and got into bed too late to keep Pearl from getting between us. Susan tried to pull the covers up, but Pearl was in the way.

"You cold?" I said.

"I don't like to lie around naked," Susan said.

"I've seen you naked five thousand times," I said.

"That's not the point," she said.

She was trying to get the covers out from under Pearl so that she could pull them over herself.

"What is the point?"

"Lying around naked is wanton," she said.

"And that's a bad thing?" I said.

"You keep peeking at me," Susan said.

"I don't peek," I said. "I stare."

Pearl moved around vigorously for a moment until she was entirely comfortable, and put her head down in a position that allowed her to look at both of us.

Susan looked at her alarm clock.

"It's ten o'clock in the morning," she said.

"On a Saturday," I said.

"And we've already had sex," she said.

"Nice start to the weekend," I said.

"And we'll probably have sex again before the weekend is over," she said.

"If we can shake Pearl," I said.

"We're grown people," she said.

"I know," I said.

"Don't you think we're oversexed?"

"You're the shrink," I said. "You tell me."

"Yes," she said. "I believe we are."

"What should we do about it?" I said.

"Encourage the pathology," Susan said, and smiled her rebel-angel smile at me.

We were quiet. The sun wasn't high enough yet to shine into Susan's bedroom window, which faced west. But the light outside the window was bright.

"Quirk wants you to help him with that Jumbo Whosis murder," she said.

"Yes."

"Why?"

"He thinks Jumbo might be getting railroaded," I said.

"Can't he stop that himself?"

"No," I said.

"He's in charge of the investigation, isn't he?"

"Officially," I said. "But there are a number of people in charge of him."

"Such as?"

"Senior command staff. Commissioner. Mayor, governor . . . and such. All of them pressured by the media."

"It's why you quit being a cop," she said.

"Some of it," I said. "But to be fair, I don't know that there is an organizational structure into which I would comfortably fit."

"Nothing bigger than you and me," Susan said. "Could he quit?"

"Quirk?" I said. "Quirk is a combination of two things. He's married and has kids. That's one thing. And he's a cop. That's the other thing. Without those, he ceases to be Quirk."

"Love and work," Susan said.

"Same as we are," I said.

"And he cares about the law," Susan said.

"He has to," I said.

"Yes," Susan said. "Doing what he does. Defining himself as he must."

"Quirk has killed people," I said. "Lot of cops never draw a weapon their whole career. Quirk has. And even if he hadn't, his business is forcing people, and preventing people, and incarcerating people."

"Without rules, the responsibility would be daunting."

"It's daunting anyway," I said. "But without rules, for a guy like Quirk, it would be impossible."

"And the law provides the rules for him," Susan said.

"Yes," I said.

I could hear a couple of mourning doves in Susan's backyard. They sounded like contentment. Pearl raised her head for a moment and stiffened her ears and listened. Then she decided they were inaccessible. Her ears relaxed and she put her head back down.

"How about you?" Susan said.

"You're the rule," I said.

"Surely there are some besides me," she said. "Some principles other than my well-being."

"Depends, I guess, on how you think about it," I said. "I know that I would sacrifice any principle for you. And I know I would not sacrifice you for anything."

"I understand that," Susan said.

I could see a couple of treetops outside the bedroom window. They were still in winter. No buds yet. But the light had become even brighter, and it was windless, and the mourning doves continued hoo-hooing.

"I'm a simple tool," I said. "I know what I like and what I don't like, and what I'm willing to do and what I'm not, and I try to be guided by that."

"And you do this difficult, sometimes dangerous, thing that you do because?"

We'd had this talk before, and never quite got the question answered. Pearl made a snuffy sound and got herself a little more comfortable at our expense.

"Because I can, I guess. Because I'm good at it."

"And because you want to see things come out right," Susan said.

"Yes," I said. "That, too."

"I'm much the same," Susan said.

"I know," I said.

ON MONDAY MORNING, Susan and I had some cheese and fruit and hot biscuits made by me before she went downstairs to shrink heads. I cleaned up the dishes, shaved, showered, and, dressed to at least the sevens, went downtown to see Rita Fiore.

I always enjoyed seeing Rita. I'd known her since she was a prosecutor in Norfolk County, and we had stayed in contact while she moved into the private practice of criminal law, and rose to a partnership in Cone, Oakes, and Baldwin. Plus, she was hot for me, and I like that in a woman.

Cone, Oakes had fifteen floors on top of a high-rise with a view of the harbor and the ocean beyond. Rita was on the top floor.

"Wow," I said when I sat down. "On a slow day you can sit and watch the planes fly in and out of Logan."

"My days aren't usually that slow," Rita said. "I understand you're working for me."

"I prefer to think of it as 'working with,' " I said.

"I'm sure you do," Rita said. "On the other hand, your pay comes through my account."

I said, "Yes, boss."

"Actually," Rita said, "I'm very glad you're aboard."

"Because I am a crackerjack detective," I said.

"That," Rita said, "and it gives me time to pursue my seduction."

"How's that worked out for you in the past?" I said.

"Not as well as I'd hoped," Rita said.

"If it's any consolation," I said, "I enjoy the attempt."

Rita shifted in her chair and crossed her legs in case I wanted to admire them. Which I did, in a sort of abstract way.

"If it's any consolation to you, you're not the only one I'm attempting," she said.

"I suspected that," I said.

"Susan's well?" Rita said.

"Susan is perfect," I said.

"Probably not," Rita said. "But I find it lovely that you think so."

"Tell me about Jumbo Nelson," I said.

"It's going to be a bitch," Rita said. "He's a perfect pig of a man, and everybody hates him, including me."

"You think he's guilty?"

"He's guilty of a lot," Rita said. "And he is such a degener- ate that it's tempting to let him take the fall for this. . . . Plus, have you seen any of his movies?"

"No. You think he killed her with malice aforethought?"

"I don't know," Rita said. "I do know that it's not clear that he did. And I do know that he has the right to the best defense available. Which is me."

"He's not been charged," I said.

"No," Rita said. "He remains a person of interest, but he's not been arrested. Some of the ADAs probably know the case isn't a lock. The way Quirk does."

"You think he will be arrested?"

"Probably," Rita said. "I think the pressure will be too much, and they'll cave."

"So you have any specific assignments for me?" I said.

"I suspect you know what to do. We'll need all we can know about the girl."

"Dawn Lopata," I said.

"Yes."

"So you'll be able to impugn her reputation if you need to."

"If we need to," Rita said. "Also, we need to know all we can about Jumbo Nelson."

"So you can counter the prosecution if they impugn Jumbo's reputation," I said.

"It's how these things sometimes work," Rita said. "But I'll bet you have found that the more you know about the princi- pals in the case, the better able you are to work the case?"

"I have found that," I said.

"Beyond that," Rita said. "I suggest you use your intelligence, guided by experience."

"Lucky I have a lot of experience," I said.

"You're too modest," Rita said.

"I know," I said.

THE LOPATA FAMILY lived in Smithfield, twelve miles north of Boston. Susan had once lived there a long time ago, when she was a guidance counselor at the junior high school, before Harvard and all that followed, so I knew my way around better than I sometimes did in the suburbs. Or wanted to.

As I drove through town, I was reminded once again of why Susan left. If you Googled "bedroom community," there'd be a link to Smithfield. It was a Saturday morning in spring, and nothing was happening. There were no kids in the school yard throwing the ball around. There was no one shopping, maybe because there was no place to shop. No dogs were racing about, no Frisbees were being thrown, no bicycles were being pedaled. The town common, which was the only evidence of New

England in Smithfield, was deserted. There weren't even any kids sitting on the wall across from the meetinghouse, smoking weed.

The Lopata home was a big style-free house in a pretentious development called Royal Acres, where there was one house to an acre, and, I suspected, no one knew anyone else. I parked on the empty street and walked up the curving brick walk to the front door. There was too little landscaping and too much house, and the recently wintered lawn stretched emptily to the next house, and the next, and the next . . . big ugly house on the prairie.

I rang the bell.

The woman who answered was wearing cropped pants and a tight top with longish sleeves pushed up on her forearms. She had a very big engagement ring, a smoker's thin face, and the blondest hair I had ever seen.

"Mrs. Lopata?" I said.

"Yeah," she said. "You the guy that called?"

"Spenser," I said.

I gave her my card.

"I'm an investigator for Cone, Oakes, and Baldwin."

"You're on their side," she said.

"Probably too early," I said, "for us and them. Mostly I'm just trying to establish what happened."

"We already got that established," she said. "The fat pervert killed my daughter."

I nodded.

"May I come in?" I said.

She shrugged.

"May as well," she said. "Better to our face than snooping around behind our back."

I smiled. These were, after all, bereaved parents.

"I may do some of that, too," I said.

She nodded absently and led me into the living room, and sat me in a brand-new flowered armchair. The room was as intimate as an operating room but not as welcoming.

She went to the living room door and yelled up the front stairs.

"Tommy, there's some kind of cop here."

"Okay."

I waited. She waited. And down the stairs he came. Pink Lacoste shirt, tan Dockers, dark brown Sperry Top-Siders.

"Spenser," he said. "Right?"

I stood.

"Right," I said.

"Memory's still hitting on all eight," he said. "Tommy Lopata."

We shook hands and sat down.

"I'm in insurance," he said. "My business to remember names."

"Own business?" I said. "Or you work for somebody."

"Independent broker," he said. "Lopata Insurance, in Malden Square."

He took a business card from a cut-glass holder on a coffee table in front of the couch and handed it to me.

"Take care of any insurance needs you got," he said. "Casualty, health, life, annuities, anything you need."

I took the card and tucked it into my shirt pocket.

"Thanks," I said.

"Buffy," he said. "How about making us some coffee?"

"Not if you're gonna drink it in here," Mrs. Lopata said. "I'm not having coffee stains on my good furniture."

"Jesus Christ, Buf," Lopata said.

"You know my rules," she said.

"I'm already over-coffeed," I said. "Thanks anyway."

She paid no attention to me while she lit a cigarette and inhaled deeply before she let the smoke ease out, as if she regretted letting it go.

"We are going to take that fat pervert for every goddamned penny he has in the world," she said.

I nodded.

"Did Dawn have any previous relationship with Mr. Nelson?" I said. "Before the night she died."

"Are you kidding?" Mrs. Lopata said. "You think I'd permit my daughter to go out with a sick tub of lard like him?"

"None that we knew of," Mr. Lopata said.

"But she went with him willingly enough that night," I said.

"Well," Mr. Lopata said. "You know, young girls, and a big movie star . . ."

"Besides which," Mrs. Lopata said, "she was some kind of sexual neurotic, anyway. I mean, the men she chased . . ."

"She have a boyfriend?" I said.

Mrs. Lopata sucked in a big lungful of smoke.

"Lots of them," Mr. Lopata said.

Mrs. Lopata made a derisive sound as she exhaled.

"That's for sure," she said.

Grief took some funny disguises. I'd talked with too many people struggling with grief to generalize about how they were supposed to do it. But the Lopatas were dealing with it more oddly than many. He was of the upbeat memory. She was a swell kid. His wife was angry. She was a slut. Maybe they were both right. The two weren't, after all, mutually exclusive.

But I was quite certain I wasn't going to penetrate either disguise today, and maybe never if I only spoke to them together.

There was a photograph on a shiny walnut credenza in front of the picture window. A young man and a young woman in their teens.

"That Dawn?" I said.

"Yes," Lopata said.

"Who's the boy?"

"Her brother," Mr. Lopata said. "Matthew."

"Where is he?" I said.

"Harvard," they said simultaneously, as if they were announcing that he was King of England.

Sometimes the temptation to amuse myself is irresistible. I nodded approvingly.

"Good school," I said.

THE STUDIO HAD RENTED a house in Wellesley for Jeremy Franklin Nelson and staff after the death of Dawn Lopata. The house had a swimming pool and tennis courts, and when I arrived with Rita Fiore, Nelson was sitting in the atrium, looking at the courts and the pool, and having a late breakfast. A Filipino man in a white jacket was serving, and a large Native American with long hair was sitting in a wicker chair in the corner of the atrium, reading the *Los Angeles Times*. There was a carafe and a coffee cup on the side table next to him.

Jumbo was still in his bathrobe, his sparse hair somewhat disorganized. Rita introduced us.

"Call me Jumbo," Nelson said. "Mean-looking fella in the

chair over there is Zebulon Sixkill. Everybody calls him Z. He's a full-blooded Cree warrior."

Z looked up from his newspaper and stared at me. I nodded at him. He remained impassive.

"Bodyguard," Nelson said. "Nobody fucks with old Jumbo when Z's around."

Z sipped from his coffee cup.

As he was talking, I was inventorying Jumbo's breakfast. He had started with a pitcher of orange juice, and now he was working on a porterhouse steak, four eggs, home fries, and hot biscuits with honey. There was a champagne flute from which Jumbo sipped between bites, and a bottle of Krug champagne was handy in an ice bucket.

"You the man going to make this cockamamie fucking legal shit go away?" Jumbo said to me.

He poured honey on a biscuit, ate the biscuit in one bite, and wiped his fingertips on his bathrobe.

"Maybe," I said.

"Whaddya mean maybe," Jumbo said. "Hot pants says you can jump over skyscrapers."

I looked at Rita. *Hot pants?*

"I'm going to see if I can find out what the truth is," I said.

Jumbo did a pretty good Jack Nicholson.

"You can't handle the truth," he said.

"I don't get to very often," I said.

"You know that line," Jumbo said.

"I do," I said.

"You know who said it?"

"I do."

"Recognize the impression?" Jumbo said.

"You bet," I said.

"Pretty good, huh?"

"Marvelous," I said. "You want to tell me about Miss Lopata?"

"I already told the fox here; she didn't tell you."

"She did," I said. "But I'd like you to go over it again."

"She is a fox, isn't she?" Jumbo said. "Hey, lemme tell you, I have wet dreams about her and I'm not even sleeping."

The Filipino houseman stepped forward and poured some more champagne into Jumbo's glass, and put the bottle back in the ice bucket.

Rita stood.

"I'm your attorney, and I'll give you the best defense I can contrive. But I'm here today as a courtesy, to introduce our investigator. I don't need to be here."

"So?" Jumbo said.

"So I'm going to wait in the car," she said, and turned and started for the door.

"This mean you don't want to fuck me?" Jumbo said.

Rita stopped and turned.

"You bet your fat ass it does," she said, and left the atrium.

Jumbo looked after her.

"Hot," he said. "Ever get a little of that?"

He cut off a chunk of steak and ate it.

"Tell me about your evening with Dawn Lopata," I said.

"First you gotta tell me about Rita," Jumbo said. "Was she as hot as she looks? She noisy? She move around a lot?"

He looked at me, popped his eyebrows like Groucho Marx, and drank some champagne.

"Jumbo," I said. "There are two things standing between you and the slam. One is your defense attorney. The other is me. You've already managed to offend her. And you are right on the verge of offending me."

With his mouth full of steak and eggs, Jumbo said, "Wha's your fucking problem?"

"There isn't a jury in the world wouldn't send you up for life if they spent five minutes with you."

"Hey, man," Jumbo said. "I don't need to listen to shit like that from some two-bit fucking peekaboo."

"Yes, you do," I said.

"You're fucking fired, then," Jumbo said. "How d'ya like them apples?"

"I don't work for you," I said. "I work for Cone, Oakes. Unless I quit."

"You better quit, because I'm gonna talk to some people," Jumbo said. "And you can take this to the bank, buddy, you'll be out on your ass."

"So what happened to Dawn Lopata," I said.

Jumbo swallowed another biscuit and drank some champagne.

"Z," he said. "Get him outta here."

The Indian stood, his face still expressionless. He jerked his thumb toward the door.

"Out," he said.

He radiated menace. I looked back at Jumbo.

"I may stay on this case just to annoy you," I said.

"Fuck you and the mule you rode in on, pal," Jumbo said.

"Plus, I'll get a chance to listen to the witty things you say."

The Indian took a step toward me. He moved oddly, as if the floor was slippery. I hated to beat a hasty retreat. But I couldn't think of anything to be gained by duking it out with Zebulon Sixkill.

So I beat a hasty retreat.

Zebulon Sixkill I

They lived in a shack with a kerosene stove, an outhouse, and no running water. As far back as he could remember, they had been a family of four: himself, his mother and father, and a bottle. They paid more attention to the bottle than they did to Zebulon. In good times, when his father worked, it would be a bottle of Jack Daniel's. In bad times, and that was mostly, it would be some sort of clear hooch with no label at all. By the time he was six, he was pretty much on his own. He was a big boy and got what he wanted by bullying the other kids in school. Somewhere in the early years, Zebulon couldn't quite remember when, his father had run off, and by the time he was eight, he already had a reputation for making trouble. By the time he was ten, his mother had died "from drinking too much," as he understood it, and he went to live with his maternal grandfather, whose name was Bob Little Bear, whom Zebulon called Bob. Bob was a widower. He spoke very little. But he didn't drink much. And when Zebulon got in trouble, Bob came down and got him and brought him home and explained to him why he shouldn't do it again. For Zebulon, Bob became a fixed beacon. He was always the same. He did what he said he'd do. He had rules, and he knew what they were and explained them to Zebulon. He taught the boy to shoot a rifle, and build a fire and cook, and generally see to himself. He explained sex to him. Zebulon found it odd to think that Bob had ever done that. Bob said he, too, found it odd, but that in fact sometimes he still did that.

"Who with?" Zebulon said.

"None of your business," Bob said.

He smiled, though, when he said it. And Zebulon could tell he was kind of proud about it. Zebulon thought for a while.

"My mother was your daughter," he said, quite suddenly.

"Yes," Bob said.

"You must have been sad when she died," Zebulon said.

"Yes," Bob said.

"I never thought of that," Zebulon said.

"No reason to," Bob said.

"You know my father?" Zebulon said.

"Yes."

"You like him?" Zebulon said.

"No," Bob said.

"I didn't like him so much, either, I guess."

"No need to," Bob said.

"You're supposed to love your father," Zebulon said.

"If he'll let you," Bob said.

"And how come they named me Zebulon?"

"After Zebulon Pike," Bob said.

"Who's he?"

"Famous explorer," Bob said. "Discovered Pikes Peak."

"Where's Pikes Peak?"

"Colorado," Bob said.

"Famous white explorer?"

"Yes."

"So how come they named me after some white person?"

"Don't know," Bob said.

"How come not a famous Cree person?"

"I don't know," Bob said.

"How come they drank all the time?"

"Don't know," Bob said.

"Why'd my father run off?"

"Don't know."

"How come you don't know anything?"

"Know we're here," Bob said. "Know we got to deal with that, and not a lot of stuff we got no way to deal with."

"Least your white-person name is easy to say."

"Easier than Zebulon," Bob said.

"WELL," RITA SAID as we drove back to Boston, "that went well."

"Can't say I've ever seen you take offense before," I said.

"Can't remember it myself," Rita said. "What did he do to offend you?"

"Asked me if I'd had sex with you."

"And you were ashamed to admit you hadn't?" Rita said.

"No, it was the way he asked," I said.

"Yes," Rita said. "There's such contempt."

"He'll be tough to defend," I said.

Rita nodded.

"Everyone on the jury will hate him," I said.

"I'd probably try to avoid a jury trial," Rita said.

"We could dump him," I said.

"Nothing would please me more, but we won't," Rita said.

"Neither one of us?"

"Neither one," Rita said. "You know it and I know it."

"I might," I said.

"Nope," Rita said. "It's ego. We both think we're the best there is at what we do."

"Well, yeah," I said.

"And we both want to know what happened in that hotel room."

"True," I said.

"It's what we do," Rita said. "Plus, you have this gallop-to-the-rescue fixation."

"Like I was telling you," I said. "I would never dump Jumbo."

"I admire that in you," Rita said. "But since we have both called him an asshole and stomped out of the room, how are we going to go about this?"

"How about Zebulon Sixkill?" I said.

"I don't like talking to him," Rita said. "He scares the hell out of me."

"Was he around that night?" I said.

"I assume so," Rita said. "He always is. They had a two-bedroom suite in the hotel. Before the studio tried to hide him out here."

"You know he was there?"

"Says he was in the living room," Rita said. "Watching television."

"Maybe I'll talk to him," I said.

"How you going to get him alone?"

"Maybe I won't," I said. "Maybe I'll have to talk with him in front of Jumbo."

"Won't Jumbo tell him to throw you out again?"

"Might," I said.

"Doesn't Zebulon Sixkill scare the hell out of you?" Rita said.

"He does," I said. "But I'll try to work around it."

"Actually, it was a silly question," Rita said. "We both know you're not afraid of him."

"No?" I said.

"You should be," she said. "But you're not."

"Why do you suppose that is?" I said.

"Because you're heroic?" Rita said.

"That would be my thinking," I said.

I SPLIT A PIZZA with Matthew Lopata in the atrium at the Holyoke Center, across from Harvard Yard. He was a serious-looking twenty-two-year-old mid-sized kid with dark hair cut short.

"My parents think me going to Harvard is like I got elected God," he said.

"You doing okay?"

"Yeah, sure," he said. "Pretty much everybody does okay, if they get in, unless they drink themselves to death."

"You graduate this year?" I said.

"Actually," Matthew said, "I graduated last year."

"Cum laude?" I said. Just to be saying something.

"Of course," he said. "You know what percentage of last year's class graduated cum laude?"

"Ninety-something," I said.

He looked a little surprised.

"That's right," he said.

"Must be the combination of highly intelligent students with great teachers," I said.

"Sure it is," Matthew said.

"You're in grad school now?" I said.

"Yeah," he said. "Economics."

"Ouch," I said.

"I know," he said. "I know, the dismal science."

He took a bite of pepperoni pizza from the narrow end of a slice.

"So how's school?" I said.

"Everybody thinks Harvard is so hard. It's no harder than anyplace else. All you got to do is study."

"Which you do," I said.

"Enough to get by," he said.

"It engages you," I said.

"Yeah," he said. "Economics is pretty interesting. I mean, the whole deal with money. Money is something we've made up, you know, because barter is clumsy. . . . It's smoke and mirrors."

"I've always suspected as much," I said. "Can we talk about your sister?"

He was quiet for a moment, looking down at the pizza. Then, without looking up, he nodded.

"Good," I said. "Tell me about her."

"Like what?" he said.

"You decide, anything comes to mind."

"She was a good kid when she was little," Matthew said. "Hell, she was always a good kid, but she was an awful mess, too."

He was still looking at the pizza.

"How so?" I said.

"My parents," he said, and shook his head. "My old man treated her like she was the carnival queen and captain of the cheerleading squad. My mother . . ." He raised his eyes from the pizza and looked at me as the conversation began to engage him. "My mother treated her like she was an ugly little slut that would fuck every guy she met."

"Which one did she buy into?" I said.

"Both," Matthew said.

It was a rainy day in Harvard Square, so the foot traffic through the atrium from Mass Ave to Mount Auburn Street was heavier than it might have been if the sun were out. A lot of people were carrying umbrellas, which most of them furled inside. I had always thought that Cambridge, in the vicinity of Harvard, might have had the most umbrellas per capita of any place in the world. People used them when it snowed. In my childhood, in Laramie, Wyoming, we used to think people who carried umbrellas were sissies. It was almost certainly a hasty generalization, but I had never encountered a hard argument against it.

"She promiscuous?" I said. "If the word still has meaning."

"Some," Matthew said. "And she was, ah, you know, bubbly and cute."

"Vivacious," I said.

"Yeah," Matthew said. "Vivacious. Worked hard as hell at it."

"She wanted to be popular?"

"More than anything."

"Maybe valued for what she was?"

"If she ever knew," Matthew said. "They really messed her up."

"Your parents?" I said.

"Yeah."

"You don't seem," I said, "at first glance, really messed up."

"I was a boy," he said.

"Different standards," I said.

"Yes," he said. "I'm two years older. I got good grades in school. When she came along, they expected that she wouldn't."

"And she didn't disappoint them."

"I guess not," Matthew said. "I played sports in high school. She didn't make cheerleader."

I nodded.

"I'm sorry to have to ask," I said. "But have any thoughts about what happened to her?"

"She probably went with him," he said. "She was impressed with movie stars."

"Even fat, piggy ones?" I said.

"It never seemed to matter," Matthew said. "If someone was interested in her, or she thought he was . . ."

"Was she interested in, ah, atypical sex?"

"Kinky stuff, you mean? I don't know how old you are, but most girls nowadays do most things."

"I'm sorry to press," I said. "But I meant things that most girls don't do nowadays."

"Stuff that might have killed her, you mean?"

"Yeah."

"Like, you know, strangulation stuff?"

"She appears to have died of asphyxiation," I said.

Matthew shook his head and looked back down at his pizza. He took a slice of pepperoni off the pizza and ate it.

"We talked some about sex," he said. "But not about that kind of stuff. You saying she coulda done it herself?"

"Or asked Jumbo Nelson to do it with her."

"He did it," Matthew said. "Didn't he? Everyone says he did."

"Don't know exactly what happened," I said. "But I will."

"Who you working for," Matthew said.

"The law firm that represents Nelson," I said.

"So you're trying to get the fucker off," Matthew said.

"Nope, that's the law firm's job. I'm just trying to find out what happened."

"And if you find out that he did it?"

"I'll tell the law firm," I said.

"And if they get him off anyway?"

"That's how the system works," I said.

"Well, the system sucks," Matthew said.

"Often," I said.

"So you're willing to let him get away with killing my sister?" Matthew said.

"I'll make that call when I have to," I said.

"Meaning?"

"Meaning it's a hard call to make. The law says if you can't convict him, then he doesn't get punished."

"And what do you say?"

"Maybe he didn't kill her. Maybe he did but it was an accident. Maybe he did it. I'll decide what to do about it when I know what happened."

"If you knew he did it, and told, would you get in trouble with the law firm?" Matthew said.

"Might."

"What firm is it?"

"Cone, Oakes, and Baldwin," I said.

"Would it matter if they were mad at you?"

"Be unlikely to hire me again," I said.

"Could they blackball you?" he said. "You know, tell other law firms?"

"Possible," I said.

"So it wouldn't be a good idea for you to tell," he said.

"It would not enhance my earning potential," I said.

Matthew was silent for a time. The pizza was mostly uneaten. The wet people came and went in the atrium. At the open ends, I could see the rain falling hard.

Then he said, "So you won't."

"Might," I said.

He repressed a scornful snort. And nodded knowingly and stood up.

"Thanks for the pizza," he said.

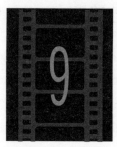

SUSAN HAD OCCASIONAL designer paroxysms in my office. Some were good. Some I didn't mind because she liked them. Occasionally an idea was inspired. The couch was inspired. Susan and I used it every now and again when we were alone in the office and going to my place or hers just seemed a long delay in our plans. Also, when Pearl was visiting she spent much of her time on it. Another winner was the small refrigerator with an ice maker, which she had set up just in back of the file cabinet where the coffeepot sat. She said it was important in case a valuable client wanted a drink. That hadn't worked out as fully as she had thought it might. But late in the day, I could sit with my chair swiveled and look out my office window, and sip scotch and soda in a tall glass with a lot of ice.

Which was what I was doing. It was nearly dark, and the rain was falling straight down, and quite a bit of it. I liked rain. I liked to listen to it. I liked to watch it. I liked to be out in it, if I was dressed for the occasion. And inside, with a drink, out of the weather, was good for feeling secure and domestic. I sat and thought, as I liked to do, about Susan and me and our time together. It always seemed to me that being with her was enough, and that everything else, good or bad, was just background noise. The rain flattened out on my window, and some of the drops coalesced into a small rivulet that ran down the glass. My drink was drunk. I swiveled around to make another one, and Martin Quirk came through my door.

"I'm off duty," Quirk said. "I can have a couple of drinks."

He took off his raincoat and shook it out, and hung it up. He took off his old-timey-cop snap-brim fedora and put it on the corner of my desk. While he was doing this, I made two drinks and handed him his.

"Soda?" I said.

Quirk shook his head.

"Rocks is good," he said. "Gimme an update."

"Scotch is Dewar's," I said." I bought it . . ."

"Jumbo Nelson," Quirk said.

"Ahh," I said. "That."

"That," Quirk said, and drank some scotch.

I told him about my visit with Jumbo and with the Lopatas, including Matthew. He listened without comment.

"So except for pissing people off," he said when I was done, "you're nowhere."

"Exactly," I said.

Quirk nodded.

"Well," he said. "You're not there alone."

"Whaddya know about Zebulon Sixkill," I said.

"Cree Indian," Quirk said. "Single. No kids. Played football at Cal Wesleyan. Worked as a bouncer. Met Jumbo while he was bouncing in a club in L.A., and Jumbo hired him. Arrested a couple times for simple assault. No other record."

"Where'd he grow up?" I said.

"Reservation in Montana," Quirk said.

"He any good?" I said.

"No idea," Quirk said. "He looks good."

"He does," I said. "Rita tells me he was in the living room of a hotel suite while Dawn Lopata was dying in the bedroom."

"Yep," Quirk said. "Heard no evil, saw no evil."

"You believe him?" I said.

Quirk shrugged.

"I assume he's sat outside a few bedrooms while Jumbo was in there," Quirk said. "He probably didn't hear anything he hadn't heard before."

"He won't talk to you," I said.

"No," Quirk said.

We sat with our scotch and didn't say anything. The rain made a quiet chatter on the windowpanes.

"Raining," Quirk said.

"Yep."

Quirk's glass was empty. He held it out to me. I made us two more. And sat and we drank some.

"You gonna talk to him?" Quirk said.

"Yes."

"How you gonna go about that," Quirk said. "You go out to Wellesley, and Jumbo will have him throw you out again."

"Thought I might visit him on the set," I said.

"While Jumbo's on camera," Quirk said.

I nodded.

"Might work," Quirk said. "Unless Zebulon bounces you on his own."

"Maybe he can't," I said.

"Maybe," Quirk said.

He tossed back the rest of his scotch, put on his hat and coat, and left.

IN THE MORNING, after breakfast, I called the Film Bureau and they told me that Jumbo Nelson's movie was shooting all day today at the Park Street Station on Boston Common.

"What's the name of the movie?" I said.

"Working title is *Oink.*"

"Perfect," I said.

So, showered, shaved, and splashed with a bouquet of after-shave, I put on jeans and sneakers, a gray T-shirt, a .38 revolver, a leather jacket and a tweed scally cap, and headed out to con-front Zebulon Sixkill. I was so clean and sweet-smelling that I decided to up my fee.

It was April 2, and it wasn't raining, but it looked like it would, as I walked across the Public Garden and across Charles Street and through the Common. At the intersection of Park and Tremont Streets, across from the Park Street Church, a block from the State House, the Park Street Station area looked like the staging site for the invasion of Normandy. There were equipment trucks, lights, trailers, honey wagons, mobile homes, a craft-services truck, some cars, extras, grips, best boys, script girls, assistant directors, production assistants, a detail cop, and a mare's nest of cables. Some spectators had gathered behind the barriers, and as I walked down into that scene, a limousine pulled up onto the corner of Tremont Street, and Jumbo Nelson, dressed like a street person, got out and walked slowly into the subway. A director yelled, "Cut!" Jumbo came back out. Got back into the limo. Shepherded by the detail cop, it backed up out of sight. Somebody held up a clacker board in front of the camera.

"Scene eighteen, take two," she said.

Somebody else, probably an assistant director, said something that sounded like "Speed?"

"Quiet on the set."

"Rolling for picture."

"And action."

The limo slid into view again as the camera tracked it. The director was looking at a small monitor as it rolled. The car stopped. Jumbo got out. An airplane went past overhead.

"Cut."

"Scene eighteen, take three."

Shepherded by the detail cop, the limo backed up out of sight. I'd been around movie sets before. They'd do this all morning. I asked a production assistant with a clipboard where I could find Zebulon Sixkill.

"He's over there," she said. "By the camera. He likes to watch the shot in the monitor."

She had blond streaks in her hair and looked to be about twenty-three. I thanked her and started over.

"Z's got kind of a short fuse."

"I'll be careful," I said.

I walked over by the camera and stood silently beside Zebulon Sixkill while Jumbo did his walk for the fifth time.

When he disappeared into the subway entrance, the director said, "Cut. It's a keeper."

Jumbo came back out.

"For crissake, Vaughn, it was five takes to get a fucking walk?"

"Want to get it right, Jumbo," the director said.

Jumbo looked at the spectators.

"Fucking directors," he said, with a lot of projection. "Won't do one take when five are almost as good."

A few spectators tittered. The director ignored him. He was already conferring with the first assistant director about the next shot.

"I'm going to craft services," Jumbo said. "Z?"

Zebulon Sixkill started after Jumbo. I went with him. As he had in Wellesley, he walked carefully, as if the ground was slippery.

"Zebulon?" I said.

He was watching Jumbo, in case some crazed fan jumped out and assaulted him for his autograph.

He said, "Call me Z."

"Okay, Z, can we talk for a few minutes?"

He looked at me.

"You," he said.

"Me."

"What the fuck?" he said.

"Wanted to ask you what happened to Dawn Lopata," I said.

"Don't know shit. Now take a walk or I'll mess you up."

"You were in the next room when she died," I said.

Jumbo saw me.

"Z, who you fucking talking to," he said.

"The asshole I threw out of Wellesley," Z said.

"So throw him off the set, too," Jumbo said. "And throw him off hard. I'm sick of him."

The detail cop was up Tremont Street, dealing with the traffic disruption that the drive up had caused. It was gonna be me and Z.

Z said, "Move it."

He put both hands on my chest and shoved me. He was strong. I took a step back.

He took me by the lapels with both hands. Up close, he smelled of booze.

Ten-thirty in the morning?

"I told you, move," he said.

I clamped my left forearm over both his hands, which pinned them to my chest. Then in a sort of leisurely way, I brought my right arm up and back and drove my elbow into his face. He bent backward. I brought the same right hand around and hit him on the right temple with the side of my clenched fist. His knees buckled. I let his hands go and pushed him away. He stumbled back a couple of steps. His head was down, and he shook it as if things weren't in place. Then he lunged at me. I put out a straight left and he ran into it, and I followed with a right cross that put him down. He was on his hands and knees. Again, he shook his head a little and started to get up. I let him. When he was on his feet, I waited. He rocked a bit, and then came at me again with a wild right hand. I checked the punch with my left hand, blocked it with my right, and slid outside the punch. I kept hold of his arm with my right, holding him at the juncture of hand and wrist so he couldn't twist loose. I pulled him slightly forward so he was off balance and hit him with three left hooks into his exposed kidney area. He gasped. I jerked him forward hard and he went down, face-first. He stayed there for a minute and then, painfully, he started to get up. I had to give him points for tough.

"Stay down," I said. "You couldn't beat me sober, and you got no chance drunk."

He got himself onto his hands and knees, almost feeling for the ground as he started to inch one leg under him.

"Z," I said. "So far I've just been discouraging you. You keep coming and I'm gonna have to hurt you."

He got both feet under him, and like someone doing a clean

and jerk too heavy for him, he forced himself upright and faced me. He put his hands up in front of his face as if he could box. Which he couldn't. He stuck a feeble left out at me. I leaned away from it. He followed with an aimless right cross, which I leaned away from in the other direction. He stood, then, with both hands up again, in front of his face. His eyes looked blank. Then, quite suddenly, without any visible volition, he sat down on the ground. Our dance was done.

"You fucking wimp," Jumbo yelled at him. "You let this fucking local keyhole sniffer kick your ass."

Z simply sat. If he heard Jumbo, he gave no sign.

"Fucking loser," Jumbo said. "When you can get your sorry ass off the ground, take a goddamned hike. I don't want to see you again. You're fired."

The detail cop came through the crowd that had gathered.

"What's going on," he said.

"My bodyguard, ex-bodyguard, is a fucking coward, that's what," Jumbo said.

"He's not a coward," I said to Jumbo. "He's hurt."

"You put him down?" the detail cop said.

"We were sparring," I said. "It got out of hand."

"My name's Ed Keohane," the cop said. "I know you?"

"Spenser," I said. "I'm a private license."

"Yeah, I know who you are," the cop said. "Aren't you pals with the homicide commander?"

"Captain Quirk," I said. "Sort of."

The cop bent over Z.

"You got anything to say?"

Z shook his head.

"You want to press charges or anything?"

Z shook his head.

"You need an ambulance?"

Z shook his head. The cop felt his pulse for a minute and straightened up.

"Anyplace he can rest, until he's got himself together?" he said.

"We could put him in Jumbo's trailer," the first AD said.

"Like hell," Jumbo said. "I'm done with him. Fucking fraud. Claimed he was tough."

"He is tough," I said. "He kept coming a long time after he should have stopped."

"So how come he's on the ground?" Jumbo said.

"He's tough enough," I said. "He just can't fight very well."

"Put him in my trailer," the director said.

The cop and I helped Z to his feet and, one on each side, we walked him to the trailer. The director opened the door and we brought him in and laid him out on the bed. The young PA I had talked to before came in.

"I'll stay with him," she said.

I looked at Z. He looked back at me. There was consciousness in his eyes. I nodded slightly and turned and left.

Outside, the ADs were getting everybody back to work. Jumbo was still there. He was eating a large cinnamon bun.

"You want a job?" he said.

"Working for you?" I said.

He took a big bite of his cinnamon bun and chewed it while he spoke.

"Good money, lotta starstruck pussy," he said.

"No," I said.

"Why not?"

"Don't like you," I said.

"Oh, fuck," Jumbo said. "Nobody likes me, but everybody likes money and snatch, and I got plenty of both. Chemicals, too, you like that."

"No," I said.

"I need a bodyguard," Jumbo said. "You're good. What'll it take."

"No," I said, and started away.

"For crissake, at least gimme a fucking reason," Jumbo said.

I paused and turned back.

"I think you're a repellent puke," I said, and walked away across the Common.

Zebulon Sixkill II

By his freshman year in high school, Zebulon was six feet two inches tall. He discovered the weight room, and by sophomore year he weighed 210 pounds and was an all-county running back. By senior year he weighed 240 and was considered the best running back in the state.

The newspapers started calling him "The Cree named Z," and the recruiters arrived in force. Bob and Zebulon talked to each of them in the neat kitchen of Bob's cabin.

The recruiter from California Wesleyan was a very rich alumnus named Patrick Calhoun who had been an all-American tackle at Cal Wesleyan thirty years ago. He was a large man, gone to fat, and very pleasant. He told Zebulon to call him Pat. He told Bob he'd be like a father to Zebulon while Z was at the university, and reminded both of them that four members of last year's Rose Bowl team had been drafted by the National Football League in the first two rounds. Zebulon and Bob talked it over for two days and opted for Pat Calhoun.

By the end of his first season he was starting as the feature back in Cal Wesleyan's pro-style offense. Pat Calhoun paid Zebulon's tuition and gave him money every week. He bought Zebulon a Mustang convertible. Bob couldn't afford to come to the games, so Pat arranged for a video of each week's game to be sent to him. Zebulon called Bob the day after every game, and they often talked for an hour. Two weeks before the beginning of Zebulon's sophomore year, Bob died. Zebulon was two weeks late coming back to college.

He sat in the football office with the head coach, Harmon Stockard, and Pat Calhoun, whom Stockard, with a smile, referred to as "one of the owners."

"I want you to take your time," Stockard said.

"You're not ready to play, that's okay. We can redshirt you for a year."

"I can play," Zebulon said.

"Z," Calhoun said, "think about it. The level we all need you to perform. It takes a ton of focus."

"I can play."

"Be sure," Stockard said. "You owe it to yourself, and you owe it to me, and you owe it to the team. We go into the season with you, and you're not ready . . ."

"I can focus," Zebulon said.

The first game he played after Bob's death he ran for 136 yards and two touchdowns.

DAWN HAD TWO FRIENDS with her the day she met Jumbo. I met them for lunch in the food court of the Galleria near Lechmere Square, close to the community college, which was just across the Gilmore Bridge. One friend was a girl with maroon hair cut short and square across her forehead. The other was a boy with an earring and one of those hairdos where it looks like you just rolled out of bed. They both wore black: jeans, sweatshirts, sneakers. The girl had on a lot of dark eye makeup. They weren't exactly goths. But they weren't a couple of management trainees, either.

When they came to my table carrying a cup of coffee each, the girl said, "Are you the detective."

"Am I sitting alone, wearing a dark blue Braves hat with a red brim and white *B* on the front?" I said.

"Yeah."

"Then it must be me," I said.

They sat down. The girl's name was Christine. The boy was James.

"My treat," I said. "You want anything."

"I just want coffee," James said.

"Just coffee," Christine said.

"Cheap date," I said. "Tell me about Dawn and Jumbo Nelson."

"You got a gun?" Christine said.

"Yep."

"On you?" she said.

"Yep."

James did a mock shiver and said, "Oooo!"

"You ever shoot anybody?" Christine said.

"Being a detective," I said, "I'm sort of used to asking the questions. Tell me about Dawn and Jumbo."

The big room was full of people, mostly adolescents, eating pizza, lamb on a skewer, and sweet-and-sour chicken with red and green maraschino cherries in it. I might have been the oldest person in the room.

"We gonna get paid for telling you stuff?" Christine said.

"No."

"I thought snitches got paid," James said.

"Not by me," I said.

Christine shrugged.

"Never hurts to ask," Christine said.

"It might," I said.

Christine shrugged again, more elaborately this time.

"We was watching them make the movie," Christine said. "And, you know, Jumbo spotted us, and come over."

James took out a pack of filter-tip cigarettes and lit one, and put the pack on the table. He inhaled deeply, held the smoke for a moment, and exhaled slowly. He held the cigarette between his first two fingers, up near the top joint.

"And he says to us, something like, how you like it so far?"

"Was he interested in Dawn right away?" I said.

"He was interested in all three of us," James said.

"You, too?" I said.

"Uh-huh."

"Was his interest carnal?" I said.

"Sure," James said.

"And you?" I said to Christine. "He interested in you?"

"Oh, yeah," she said. "Me and Dawn."

"And it was carnal?"

"You mean did he want us to screw him?" Christine said. "Yeah, sure. He wanted to hook up with all three of us."

"He say so?"

"Uh-huh," James said.

He took a card from his pocket and put it face up on the table. Christine took out a card just like it. On the front it said

"Jumbo." I turned the cards over. The hotel name and room number were written on the back, along with a phone number.

"That's his cell phone number," James said.

"Dawn got one, too?" I said.

"Sure," Christine said.

She picked up James's cigarettes, took one, put it in her mouth, and leaned toward James. He lit it for her, and she inhaled and let the smoke out slowly, with her lower lip forward so the smoke drifted up in front of her face. Dramatic. I wondered how often she'd practiced. It was odd to sit with two people smoking. I had quit years ago, and it was odd even to see people smoking. Smoking was mostly something done by some shivering isolate outside an office building in the winter.

"He focus in on her?" I said.

"Nope," James said. "He was ready for any of us."

I said, "It doubles the dating pool, I guess."

"You interested?" James said.

"No."

"You don't find me attractive?" James said.

"Stunning," I said. "But not my type."

"What's your type?" James said.

He was having fun.

"Female," I said.

"You married?" Christine said.

"I keep steady company with the girl of my dreams," I said.

"So I don't interest you, either?" she said.

"Sadly," I said, "no."

"Because of your girlfriend?"

"Exactly," I said.

In fact, of course, I had never been aroused by anyone with maroon hair.

"That's amazing," Christine said.

James grinned.

"Old school," he said.

"So how come Dawn was the one ended up in Jumbo's hotel room?" I said.

"Too fat for me," James said.

He dropped his cigarette butt on the floor and stepped on it.

"Christine?" I said.

She squinched up her face.

"Gross," she said.

"But Dawn liked him?" I said.

"Dawn wasn't choosy who she hooked up with," James said.

He lit a new cigarette.

"And for crissake," Christine said, "he was a freaking movie star. You know?"

"She would care about that?" I said.

"Of course," Christine said. "Who wouldn't."

"You?" I said.

"Sure," she said. "But he's too icky."

"But not too icky for Dawn," I said.

"No."

"Why not," I said.

They were silent for a moment. James let the smoke from his new cigarette drift out through his nose.

"Not many people too icky for Dawn," he said.

I looked at Christine. She shrugged.

"Dawn wasn't choosy," she said. "She was a good kid, but she, you know, went for pretty much anybody with a winkie."

"A winkie?" I said.

"You know," Christine said.

I nodded.

"So what do you think happened with her and Jumbo?" I said.

She shrugged and took another cigarette from James's pack. He lit it for her.

"I think it was kinky sex, got out of hand," James said.

"Anything special?" I said.

"Said in the papers that she died of asphyxiation," James said.

"I know," I said.

"That right?" he said.

"They're not sure," I said.

"Well, if it is . . ." James spread his arms as if it was a no-brainer.

"She into choking games?" I said.

"Got me," James said.

"Christine?" I said.

"I don't know," Christine said. "She was very interested in all kinds of sex stuff."

"Aren't we all," I said.

"We're kids," James said. "We're even more interested."

"Ageist," I said.

"And," Christine said, "I think she might have been more interested than most."

I STOPPED ON MY WAY back to the office to get a sub sandwich. When I got back to my office, it was nearly two in the
afternoon. I found Zebulon Sixkill, fragrant with booze, asleep
on the floor in front of my office. I stepped over him, unlocked
my door, and opened it. I put my sandwich on my desk and
went back and got hold of Zebulon Sixkill by the collar and
dragged him into the office and laid him out on my office rug.
I stepped back over him again and shut my office door, then
made some coffee, poured myself a cup, and sat at my desk with
my feet up, eating my sandwich and drinking my coffee. When
I got through, I wrote some bills and put them in envelopes
and stamped them.

At about three-thirty the sun had moved out over the Charles

River, five blocks away. It slanted in through my office window, making a long parallelogram on the floor where Zebulon Sixkill was lying on his back. It woke him up.

"Where the fuck am I," he said.

His voice was very hoarse.

"My office," I said.

"Who the fuck are you?"

"Spenser," I said. "We met, couple days ago."

He raised his head and looked at me. I smiled in a friendly way.

"Yeah," he said. "You got a bathroom?"

I pointed. He got painfully up and went into the bathroom. He was in there a long time. When he came out he looked as if he might have washed his face.

I pointed to a chair.

"You got a drink?" Zebulon Sixkill said.

I took the bottle of Dewar's out of my desk drawer and put it on the desk along with a lowball glass. He took a couple of deep breaths as if to steady himself and carefully poured some. He looked at the glass for a moment, then picked it up with both hands and drank some whiskey. He showed no sign of pleasure. He drank it the way you take aspirin for a headache.

"You're lucky," I said. "Lila across the hall had seen you, she'd have called the cops and you'd be waking up in the drunk tank."

"That's me," Zebulon Sixkill said. "Lucky."

"You functional?" I said.

"I will be in a minute," he said. "You got any ice?"

"Wow," I said. "A picky drunk."

SIXKILL

I got him some ice in a second lowball glass. He poured the
remains of his drink over it and drank some. I waited. He sat.

After a while he said, "I'm in trouble."

I nodded.

"I can see that," I said.

He shook his head and poured a little scotch over the ice in
his glass.

"All my life I been a tough guy. You know?"

"Till now," I said.

Z looked at me. I looked back.

"Whaddya want?" I said finally.

He shook his head again. We sat. He drank a little of his
drink.

"I never lost a fight before," he said.

"Have many?"

"People always careful around me."

"Ever fight somebody knew what they were doing?" I said.

He held his glass of whiskey and looked at it some more.

"Guess not," he said.

We were quiet again. He drank a little. I was watching
something happening. I wasn't sure what. But I kept watching.

"You know what you're doing," he said.

"Yep."

"I want you to show me how," he said.

"If you don't get the booze under control, it's a waste of
time," I said.

"I can not drink," he said.

"You just got no reason not to," I said.

"No," he said.

"You been juicing?"

"Like HGH?" he said. "That kind of thing?"

"Yeah."

"Little," he said.

"Rock bottom," I said.

"Yeah."

We sat for a time, contemplating how rock-bottom he was. Finally I said, "Good place to start."

"Good as any," he said.

Zebulon Sixkill III

Her name was Lucy, and he'd never seen anything like her. She was a Southern California sorority girl, and she was the color of honey. Golden hair, golden tan. Golden prospects. She was homecoming queen during his second season. The first time they had sex, he discovered that her golden tan was all over. He loved that. He loved the fresh smell of her. Expensive soap. Shampoo. Cologne. She always sat close to him. She always looked right at him when he talked. Her lips were glossy and parted slightly when she listened to him. She was rapturous when they made love, and she was always waiting outside the locker room after a game. He could talk to her. He talked about his parents, and their friend Mr. Booze. About his grandfather, and the loss of him. About being a Cree. They went together to dinners at Mr. Calhoun's home in Bel Air. On the weekends they went to uproarious parties at Mr. Calhoun's place in Malibu. They clubbed on Sunset. They came to know a lot about good wine and fine whiskey. They became increasingly sophisticated about which drug to use for which effect. Their pictures were in the style section. Paparazzi began to notice them coming out of clubs. At the end of sophomore year, they moved into a condo owned by Mr. Calhoun, near the campus.

Zebulon loved her so intensely that he felt somehow submerged in it. He saw everything through the golden haze of it. He felt as if he were fully breathing for the first time. When he was small and lived with his mother and father, they were mostly drunk, or gone. He remembered feeling mostly afraid. He had felt safe with Bob. He admired Mr. Calhoun, and he respected Coach Stockard. But Lucy was something he had no words for. She seemed to contain him, to roll over him like surf. She seemed to be reality. And nothing else did.

"WHERE IS HE NOW?" Susan said.

We were having breakfast in the café at the Taj hotel, which used to be the Ritz. Our table was in the small bay that looks out on Newbury Street, and the spring morning was about perfect.

"He's asleep on my couch," I said.

"You've taken him in," Susan said.

"For the moment," I said.

"Good God," Susan said.

I smiled becomingly.

"Sometimes," Susan said, "I think you are far too kind for your own good."

I ate a bite of hash.

"And some other times?" I said.

"I think you are the hardest man I've ever seen," she said.

"So to speak," I said.

"No sexual allusion intended," Susan said.

She broke off the end of a croissant, put very little strawberry jam on it, and popped it in her mouth.

"Do I have to be one or the other?" I said.

She finished chewing her croissant, and touched her mouth with her napkin.

"No," she said, "you don't. And in fact, you are both. But it's an unusual combination."

"So are we," I said.

Susan smiled.

"We surely are," she said.

"But a good one," I said.

"Very good," Susan said. "What are you going to do with him?"

"Try and fix him," I said. "After all, he might be able to help me with Dawn Lopata."

"Ah," Susan said. "A practical purpose."

"Keeps me from being a do-gooder," I said.

Susan nodded.

"Successfully," she said. "I'm sure you can get him in shape and teach him to box and all, if he sticks with you. Do you think you can get him off the booze?"

"I don't think he's an alcoholic," I said.

"Why?"

"Informed guess," I said. "You ever work with alcoholics?"

"People become dependent on alcohol for many different reasons," Susan said. "If the reasons are amenable to psychotherapy, sometimes I can help."

"Such as?" I said.

"Reasons?" she said. "Oh, childhood abuse leading to feelings of low self-worth, maybe. Whatever it is, for me, it is a process of curing the whole person."

"Not everyone wants that," I said. "Some of them just want to stop drinking."

"And they perhaps go elsewhere."

"And if they stop drinking, they're still the same person they were, except they don't drink," I said.

"Possibly," Susan said.

"But doesn't what caused them to drink in the first place remain undisturbed?"

"Might," Susan said.

"And maybe work its way out in another form?" I said.

"Could," Susan said.

"Try not to be so dogmatic about this," I said.

She smiled. Which was like moonlight on the Seine.

"We are both in uncertain professions," Susan said.

She shrugged.

"Can't hurt if I train him," I said.

"Probably can't," Susan said. "But you might wish to remind yourself that people develop a means of coping with stress, and, even after the stress is gone, the coping mechanism is there and working."

"Which can cause a lot of trouble," I said.

"A lot," Susan said.

"On the other hand," I said, "you gotta start somewhere."

"Or," Susan said, "you could tell him to peddle his problems someplace else."

"I think I'll start somewhere," I said.

"There's a shock," Susan said.

THE INN ON THE WHARF was a new boutique hotel for the very uppermost crust, which translated roughly into those who could afford it. It was on the waterfront, and all rooms had a view of the harbor. The top-floor suites, where Jumbo had been, probably had a view of Lisbon.

I was off the lobby, in a windowless little office, talking to the director of hotel security, a former FBI agent named Dean Delmar. Hotel counsel was also present.

"Nice view," I said.

Delmar shrugged.

"Our job is not ostentatious," he said.

"I can see that," I said. "What can you tell me about the night Dawn Lopata died?"

"I went over this with a couple of detectives already," Delmar said. "Can't you just access their notes?"

"I like to start from scratch," I said. "That way, my mind is uncluttered, so to speak."

"We have no legal obligation to tell you anything," Hotel Counsel said.

He looked like someone from casting had sent him over to play the corporate lawyer. He was youngish, and lean, with dark hair cut short and a pair of blue-framed half-glasses that he wore low on his nose, so he could look over them at you.

"Of course you don't," I said. "But I know that both of you, like good citizens everywhere, want this terrible incident resolved, and would prefer it be resolved with a minimum of media attention."

"Are you threatening to involve the media if we don't talk with you?" Hotel Counsel said.

"Are you suggesting that I am the kind of sleazy gumshoe that would do such a thing?" I said.

We looked at each other.

"Let us agree," Hotel Counsel said, "that what is said here stays here."

"Is there a big secret?" I said.

"No," Hotel Counsel said. "Of course not. But I don't want any loose talk besmirching the hotel."

"No besmirching," I said.

"It is not a frivolous request," Hotel Counsel said. "The

public perception of this hotel can mean the difference between success and failure."

"I am employed by Cone, Oakes, and Baldwin," I said. "I will share what I learn with them."

"And no one else."

"Within the guidelines of legality," I said.

Hotel Counsel glanced at Delmar and shrugged and nodded.

"Whaddya need?" Delmar said to me.

"Run through it for me," I said. "When did you first learn that something was amiss in Jumbo Nelson's suite?"

"Call to the front desk, around eleven-thirty," Delmar said.

"From?"

"Not entirely clear," Delmar said. "Best guess is the bodyguard."

"Zebulon Sixkill," I said.

"Yep."

"Could it have been Jumbo?" I said.

"Clerk said she thought it was the Indian," Delmar said. "But it was sort of a crisis call, so she may be wrong."

"In public," Hotel Counsel said, "you might not want to refer to him as 'the Indian.' The bodyguard is all right. Or Mr. Sixkill. But not 'the Indian.'"

"You bet," Delmar said.

"What did the caller say?" I asked.

"Said there was a medical emergency and to call an ambulance," Delmar said.

"Which you did."

74

"Of course, and the desk clerk called me and I sent a couple of my people up; one had EMT training. The Indian . . . The bodyguard let them in. Found the girl lying on her back on the bed."

"Clothed?" I said.

"Yes," Delmar said. "My guys couldn't get a pulse. They tried to resuscitate her, but . . ." He spread his hands. "One of them called me, said he thought she was dead. I said, 'Of what?' He said he didn't know. I called the cops."

"Where was Jumbo?" I said.

"Sitting in the living room," Delmar said. "Fully dressed."

"Doing what?" I said.

"Nothing," Delmar said. "My guys said he just sat there."

"Say anything?" I asked.

"Nope."

I looked at Hotel Counsel.

"Mr. Sixkill speak?" I said.

"No," Delmar said. "Not a word."

"And then the city arrived," I said.

"Ambulance came," Delmar said. "Cops came, and it was pretty well out of our hands after that."

"Theories?" I said.

"I think they were having rough sex and it got out of hand," Delmar said.

"That is, of course, Mr. Delmar's personal speculation only," Hotel Counsel said.

"You weren't quoting somebody else?" I said to Delmar.

Delmar smiled faintly.

"Just so we're clear," Hotel Counsel said.

"They took her to Boston City?" I said.

"Yes," Delmar said.

"May I talk with the two hotel security people who first went up to the room?"

"I prefer all discussion to go through Mr. Delmar and myself," Hotel Counsel said.

"I prefer that you be less of a horse's ass," I said.

"No need to be abusive," Hotel Counsel said.

"Just so we're clear," I said.

ZEBULON SIXKILL AND I went to the Harbor Health Club in the early afternoon. He looked great in a black tank top and sweats. The muscles in his arms and shoulders were startling, and bulged or relaxed smoothly with every movement. People looked at him when he came, the way people often looked at Hawk. Being a trained investigator, I concluded that he'd probably done some weight work.

"How much can you bench, Zebulon?"

"Z," he said.

"Got it," I said. "How much do you bench."

"Four-fifty," he said.

"Let's start with half that," I said.

"No fighting?" Z said.

"We will," I said. "Just see how many reps you can do with two-twenty-five. The machine is fine."

Z nodded and slid into the reclining bench-press machine and set the pin at two-twenty-five and did fifteen reps.

"How many can you do?" Z said.

I shrugged and got into the machine and did twenty-five.

"Jesus Christ," Z said.

"On the other hand," I said. "I've never done four-fifty in my life."

Z nodded.

"Different approach," I said. "You run?"

"Ten miles," Z said.

"Ever do intervals?"

"Fast and slow?" Z said.

"Sort of," I said.

"Football," he said.

I nodded.

Mostly in deference to Hawk and me, and also with a nod to his own years as a ranked lightweight, Henry Cimoli had salvaged a boxing room when the club went upscale. Z and I went in, away from the bright, tight workout clothes and the mirrors and the chrome weight machines, and the upbeat listen-while-you-sweat music. There was a speed bag, a heavy bag, a little two-ended jeeter bag that even Hawk had trouble with, a couple of body bags, and an open space with rubber floor mats for sparring.

Henry Cimoli came in wearing a white satin sweat suit. And custom sneakers.

"Thought I saw you come in," Henry said. "New sparring partner?"

"Sort of," I said. "Henry, this is Z. Z, Henry."

They shook hands. When they finished, Henry shook his as if it hurt.

"Nice grip you got there, Z," Henry said.

Z nodded.

"Hawk still in East Bumfuck?" Henry said to me.

"Central Asia," I said.

"When's he coming home," Henry said.

"Whenever he wants to," I said.

Henry nodded.

"That would be Hawk," he said. "You guys gonna box?"

"I'm conducting a little introduction for Z," I said. "Wanna sit in?"

"He want to be a pro or just win the fights in the alley?"

"Alley," Z said.

"Probably win most of those now, being so big and strong," Henry said.

"Wanna win all," Z said.

"But no one ever taught him," I said to Henry.

Henry looked at Z.

"Okay," Henry said. "I fought at one-thirty-two. Long time ago. I weigh about one-forty-five now. And, if you don't know, I'd clean your clock."

Z shook his head.

"Can he take a punch?" Henry asked me.

"Yes."

"You've tested that?"

"Yes."

Henry nodded.

"Wanna try it?" he said.

"Me and you?" Z said.

"Sure, open hand, we'll just slap. Nobody gets hurt."

Z looked at me.

"It'll be instructive," I said. "You won't hurt him."

He shrugged.

"Right here?" he said.

"Sure," Henry said. "That'll be your corner. This'll be mine. Spenser will ref."

"No need to worry about hitting him below the belt," I said to Z. "He's so short nobody can reach that low."

Z stood in his corner.

I said, "Bong!"

Henry went into his fighting stance. Left foot forward, knees bent, hands high on either side of his face. Z came from his corner with his hands held loosely a little above his waist. He put out a left jab at Henry, who moved around it. Z followed with a right cross, and Henry moved around it. They went around the room that way for more than a minute, with Z throwing open-handed punches, and Henry bobbing and weaving just enough to make him miss.

Z was breathing hard.

"Stay still," he said.

Henry grinned at him.

"Okay," he said, and stopped.

Z closed with him. Henry leaned and rolled and bobbed without moving his feet and Z still couldn't hit him. Z was arm-weary. His hands were low. He tried a left. Henry checked it with his right, and stepped around it. Henry put two open-right-hand punches into the body, and as Z wheeled toward him, Henry put an open left hook onto Z's chin. Z shook his head and tried a right. Henry checked it with his left hand and put an overhand left onto Z's jaw. Z lunged at Henry, trying to grab him. Henry put out a left jab that Z ran into, and then rolled around Z so that he was behind him. He hit him a couple of times in the kidneys. And as Z turned wearily, his hands down, his voice rasping, Henry slapped him left, right, left, right on the cheeks.

"Bong," I said.

Z stared at Henry.

"Annoying," I said. "Isn't it."

"Do that to you?" Z said.

"No," Henry said. "I couldn't. He knows how. He's as quick as I am, and he's in shape."

"And me?" Z said.

"You, Kemo Sabe, are quick enough," Henry said. "But you don't know how and you're not in shape."

"Kemo Sabe?" Z said, and looked at me.

"Henry speaks many languages," I said.

Z studied Henry for a minute.

"You're a big, strong guy," Henry said. "And you got nice natural reflexes. I don't want to close with you until you're ready to puke."

"No wind," Z said.

Henry nodded.

"And you don't know how to fight," Henry said. "Ever been a bouncer?"

"Yeah."

"Figures, they like guys like you," Henry said. "Big, scary. Stop a lot of fights before they start."

"And most of them are drunk," Z said.

"Like you were," I said. "When we fought."

"Drunk's never an asset in a fight," Henry said.

"I don't need to be drunk," Z said.

"Sure," Henry said. "Guy like you . . . You grab some guy, don't know any more than you. You slam him up against a wall, give him one big punch on the side of the head. Fight over."

Z nodded.

"Been winning fights all my life," Z said. "Never had a problem until the other day."

Henry nodded toward me.

"Then you ran into him?" Henry said. "And he knew more than you."

Z nodded.

"Well," Henry said. "There you go."

Zebulon Sixkill IV

After the second game of his junior year, Harmon Stockard called Zebulon into the football office.

"What's going on, Z?" he said.

"What?" Zebulon said.

"Coach Brock says you're not in the weight room much anymore, and when you do show up, you dog it."

"I work hard, Coach," Zebulon said.

"They tell me you are ten pounds heavier than you were last spring."

Zebulon shrugged.

"Against Oregon last week you carried twenty-eight times and gained forty yards. Against Michigan this week, you carried twenty-three times and gained fifty-one yards."

Zebulon didn't say anything.

"You used to explode into the line," Stockard said. "You hit the hole so quick Turk had to hurry to get the handoff out there."

Zebulon was silent.

"Now the hole closes before you get to it."

"Maybe guys aren't holding their blocks," Zebulon said.

"Hell they aren't," Stockard said. "Turk's turned and holding the ball and looking for you and here you come

a step later. It's all it takes. It's the difference between everything and nothing."

Zebulon looked at Stockard and looked away. He didn't speak.

"You are throwing it away, kid," Stockard said. "You were a first-round lock."

Zebulon shrugged.

"I'm going to start Rollie next week," Stockard said. "I'm gonna sit you until you're ready to play."

Zebulon nodded. They both sat for a moment. Then Stockard got up and came to stand in front of Zebulon.

"Goddamn it, Z, you're special, you got a chance to be Riggins, Csonka, Jimmy Taylor."

Zebulon didn't know who those men were.

"Don't let it go," Stockard said. "Most people never get the chance. You got the chance. Don't let it go."

Zebulon shook his head as if there was something in his ear. He stood, and in standing, pushed Stockard a step back from him.

"Fuck this," Zebulon said.

He walked out of the office. Stockard watched him go. Kid was the best he ever coached. Stockard wanted to save him but didn't know how. He couldn't let one of his players shove him, for crissake. Kid was always kind of sullen. No, that wasn't fair. Kid was always very quiet. No excitement. He was so good. It came so easy. But he seemed to have no rah-rah. Play this game, you needed a little rah-rah. Rollie wasn't as good as Z. No one was. But Rollie was good. And he was excited with it. And excited with the game. Maybe if it wasn't so easy for Z. After the Arizona State game, Stockard took a deep breath and cut him.

IT WAS KIND OF COLD for a picnic, so Susan and I sat in the
front seat of my car and ate submarine sandwiches and looked
at the river from a parking lot near WBZ. That is to say, I ate
my sandwich. Susan deconstructed hers and ate it like a com-
posed salad from the wrapper in her lap.

"Did you arrange for Henry to be there?" Susan said. "Or was
it serendipity?"

"Serendipity," I said.

Susan plucked a small slice of pickle from the sandwich and
ate it.

"Well, it was fortuitous," she said when she had finished
chewing. "Don't you think?"

"Susan," I said. "If you keep talking like you went to Harvard, I may be forced to withhold sex."

"When's the last time you did that?" Susan said.

"Well," I said. "I haven't ever had to actually withhold. The threat was always enough."

"Besides," Susan said. "I did go to Harvard."

"Well, I suppose that gives you a mulligan," I said.

Susan said, "Whew," and carefully ate a tomato slice.

There were a lot of high clouds in the sky, and the river was gray in the raw spring light, and it moved past, without seeming to, at a pretty good clip. The college crews were out. But they seemed always to be out, except when the river was frozen. There were recreational rowers, too. I ate some of my sandwich. Susan took a bite off of the edge of a cold cut.

"How did he take it?" Susan said. "When Henry showed him up?"

"Z? Not bad. Like he took it when I beat him. He was startled and then puzzled, except with Henry he wasn't drunk."

"What time of day?" Susan said.

"Early afternoon," I said.

"Many people are not drunk in the early afternoon," Susan said.

"But some are," I said. "And this particular early afternoon, he wasn't."

Susan nodded.

"And he gave you no excuses?"

"No. He'd been beaten, and he knew it."

"He wants you still to train him?"

"He does," I said.

"And you will," Susan said.

"Yes. Try to get him in shape, too."

"Has he told you anything new about that girl's death?" Susan said.

"I haven't asked," I said.

"Why not?" Susan said.

I shrugged.

Susan looked at me while she nibbled another quarter-inch bite off the edge of the cold cut.

"Because you don't want him to think you're training him just to get information," Susan said.

"That's probably correct," I said.

"Are you?" Susan said.

"Training him so he'll tell me stuff?"

"Yes."

"I'm training him for several reasons," I said.

"Is information one of them?" Susan said.

"It is," I said.

Susan smiled and patted my thigh.

"You wouldn't be you if it weren't," she said.

"We wouldn't want that," I said.

"No, we wouldn't," Susan said. "But you also want to help him."

"You think?" I said.

"Does anyone know you like I do?"

"I hope not," I said.

"He wants to be a tough guy," Susan said. "He's come to the right place."

"I can't teach him how to be a tough guy," I said. "I can teach him how to fight. But he'll have to be tough on his own."

"I know," Susan said.

"You're as tough as I am," I said.

"I know that, too," Susan said.

"But you wouldn't win many fistfights," I said.

"Depends who I was fighting," Susan said.

"Yes," I said. "I guess it would."

"And you would win a lot of fistfights," she said.

"Depends who I was fighting," I said.

Susan smiled and nibbled on a fragment of her sandwich. Mine had long ago disappeared. I was drinking coffee from a large paper cup.

"Winning fistfights means being good at fistfighting," Susan said. "Being tough means looking straight at something ugly, and saying, 'That's ugly; I'll have to find a way to deal with it.' And doing so."

"By that definition, most people in their lives have a chance to be tough," I said.

"And aren't," Susan said.

"And we are," I said.

"It's sort of how we make our living," Susan said. "Each in our own way."

"Shouldn't that be 'each in *his* own way'?" I said.

"Not when we're talking about me," Susan said.

"If you say so, Ms. Harvard Ph.D.," I said.

Susan smiled again. I would be quite happy to sit around and watch her smile, for nearly ever.

"Couple of tough guys," I said.

Susan's smile widened.

"Are we a pair?" she said.

I WENT TO THE LOBBY of the Inn on the Wharf and sat
down in a designer armchair, and waited. If I sat there long
enough, someone from security would come over and ask me
if I was a guest at the hotel. It took a bit more than an hour of
sitting before a slightly stocky blonde woman in a dark blue
pantsuit came over. She wore a small earpiece, like they do.

"Excuse me, sir," she said. "Are you a guest of the hotel?"

"No, ma'am," I said. "I want to talk to someone in security,
but I don't know who is or isn't, you know?"

"So you came here and sat and assumed after a while someone
from security would present themselves," she said.

"Exactly," I said.

"Why didn't you ask at the desk?" she said.

"Been told by a lawyer," I said, "that I'm not supposed to talk with you."

"Really? What lawyer?"

"Never got his name," I said. "Hotel Counsel."

She shrugged.

"Why do you want to talk with someone from security?" she said.

"I'm a detective," I said. "Working on the Dawn Lopata case."

"Who you work for," she said.

The polished public self was beginning to wear away, revealing the presence of an actual person.

"I'm private," I said. "Right now I'm working for Cone, Oakes, and Baldwin."

"The law firm?"

"Yes. They're defending Jumbo Nelson."

"Pig," she said.

"Agreed," I said. "But is he a guilty pig? I'd like to talk to the first people into the room after he called down."

"I was one," she said.

"What's your name?" I said.

"Zoë," she said. "Zoë Foy."

"Sit down, Zoë," I said. "Tell me what you saw."

"Against the rules to sit with a guest," she said. "The big Indian let me in. It's a suite. Jumbo is there, in the living room, sipping some champagne."

"Dressed?" I said.

"Wearing some kind of velour sweat suit, 'bout size one hundred."

"Shoes?"

"The stupid-looking flip-flop slippers the hotel provides," she said. "Me and Arnie—Elmont, the other security person—go right past them into the master bedroom and she's on the bed, fully clothed, lying on her back, with her hands at her sides."

"Bed made?" I said.

"Yeah," she said. "Rumpled, but the spread was still on."

"Was she alive?" I said.

She shook her head.

"When I was on the job in Quincy," she said. "I had some EMT training. Me and Arnie could see right away she was cooked. But I tried resuscitating her, until the ambulance arrived."

"No luck?"

"Nope."

"They took her to Boston City?" I said.

She smiled faintly.

"Boston Medical Center," she said.

"I'm old school," I said. "Anything else you saw that matters?"

"Fatso looked a little worried," she said. "The Indian didn't look anything. Nobody looked, you know, like, sad that this kid had died."

"You think they knew she was dead?"

"She didn't look alive," Zoë said.

"Anything else?" I said.

She shook her head. I took my card from a shirt pocket and gave it to her.

"If you or Arnie have any recollections of interest," I said, "give me a call."

"The pig did it, you know," Zoë said.

"You sure?" I said.

"Creepy bastard," Zoë said.

"Be nice if we could hang it on him," I said. "But maybe he didn't."

She shrugged.

"Idle question?" I said.

"Sure."

"How come you were willing to talk with me after I told you Hotel Counsel said no?"

Zoë smiled.

"Fuck him," she said.

THE ER DOCTOR who had worked on Dawn Lopata when they brought her in was a young guy named Cristalli. I talked with him in an examining room near the triage desk.

"She was dead when she got here," he said. "We tried, why wouldn't we? But she was unresponsive."

"Which is medical speak for dead," I said.

"Just like *discomfort,*" he said, "is medical speak for pain."

"You have a thought about what killed her?" I said.

"I'm not the ME," he said. "But we see a lot of death from trauma coming through here, and I'd say she was strangled."

"You have a theory as to how?"

"Ligature," he said.

"How long before she would have lost consciousness?" I said.

"Ten, fifteen seconds," he said.

"And death?"

"Minutes," Dr. Cristalli said.

"So you'd need to keep the pressure on even after the vic loses consciousness," I said.

"If it's death you're after," he said.

"So can it happen accidentally?" I said.

"Sure. We regularly get people who strangle themselves playing choking games, usually masturbatory."

"You can tell?" I said.

"That it was masturbatory?"

"Yeah," I said.

"It's usually pretty obvious at the death scene," Dr. Cristalli said.

"It is?" I said. "Like how . . . Never mind."

"Never mind?" Cristalli said.

"I can guess, and it's all I want to do," I said.

"Anyway," Cristalli said. "In this case, EMTs told me there was no sign of it."

"She was fully dressed," I said. "Lying on her back on the bed."

"That's what they told me," he said.

"Presumably she'd been having sex," I said. "Odd that she'd be fully dressed."

"I didn't check," Cristalli said. "Once it was clear that she wasn't coming back, she became a problem for the ME."

"So you don't know if she was having sex or not," I said.

"Nope," he said. "But there are a couple things about that,

and I admit I wouldn't have registered it. One, she wasn't wearing a bra."

"Not everyone does," I said.

"Nurses insist that she would have."

"Well-endowed?" I said.

"Excessively, I would say, but it is, I suppose, a matter of personal preference."

"What's the other thing?" I said.

"Her underpants were on backward."

"Backward," I said. "I'm not sure I could tell."

"That's what they told me," he said.

I nodded. We were quiet. Outside the exam room, a stretcher came in and stopped at the desk.

"Somebody dressed her," I said.

"The thought occurred," he said.

Zebulon Sixkill V

The deal was, Pat Calhoun said, "I take care of the money. You take care of the football."

Zebulon nodded.

"Well," Pat said. "You're not taking care of the football no more."

They were sitting in the red-leather front seat of Pat's silver Mercedes in a parking lot in Garden Grove.

Zebulon was silent.

"Looking back, I realize," Pat said, "that I'm at

fault. I promised your grandfather I'd look after you, and . . . hell, I guess I trusted you too much."

Zebulon shrugged.

"You stopped running your sprints. You stopped pumping your iron. You weren't focused on the game. Hell, Harmon says you forgot half the plays; it's the same offense you ran in last year."

Zebulon nodded. Pat shook his head.

"Too much booze, too much dope, too many prom queens."

"Just Lucy," Zebulon said.

"Sure," Pat said. "Too much fucking."

"Don't talk about Lucy," Zebulon said.

"Right, sorry," Pat said. "Anyway, you're out of shape, you're off the team, and I am not paying your way anymore."

"How do I pay tuition?" Zebulon said.

"Ain't that a good question," Pat said. "How you gonna eat, for crissake?"

"Need a job," Zebulon said.

"You do, and because I feel guilty, like I let your grandfather down, I'm gonna give you one. I own a club in Hollywood. They can use a bouncer. Big, tough guy like you. Good-looking don't hurt with the ladies. Don't know what they're paying, but I'll see to it you get enough to keep you going."

"How about the condo," Zebulon said.

"Gonna sell it," Pat said. *"I'll give you a month to find another place."*

"Where's the club?" Zebulon said.

"Sunset, west of Highland."

"What time?"

"Tomorrow night, nine o'clock. Wear black pants and a black T-shirt."

Zebulon nodded.

"Okay," he said.

HARVARD STADIUM LOOKED like a smaller version of the Roman Colosseum. Z and I were in the stadium, on the empty football field. We who are about to kick off salute you.

"How far can you sprint?" I said.

"I can run a ways," Z said.

"How far can you do it full-out, like you were running the hundred."

"We did forties when I was playing football."

"Okay," I said. "We'll run some intervals. Sprint one hundred yards, walk two hundred. Sprint one hundred, walk two hundred. See how it works out."

Z shrugged. We walked to the goal line.

I said, "Go," and we sprinted for the other end zone. At the fifty, Z began to flag. And I was waiting for him in the end zone when he came slowly across the goal line, breathing very hard.

"Now we walk back, and then walk back here, and then sprint another one hundred," I said.

"Sure," Z said.

We walked the two hundred at an easy pace. And sprinted one hundred. And walked two hundred. After the eighth sprint, Z threw up.

"Hey," I said. "You're in Harvard Stadium."

Bent over with his hands braced on his thighs, he gasped, "Outta shape."

We sat in the empty stands for a bit while Z's health returned.

"I thought I was in shape," Z said. "I thought I could fight."

"Confusing," I said. "You sure you're a Cree Indian?"

"What they told me," Z said.

"Good," I said. "If you were Irish, Sixkill would be a really funny name."

"Sounds better in Cree," he said.

"Lemme hear," I said.

He said something.

"By God, you're right," I said.

"What about that girl?" he said.

"Know anything?"

Z shrugged.

"I was in the living room," he said. "Jumbo opens the bedroom door, tells me to call."

"He have many guests like that in his room?"

"Every day," Z said.

"Always girls?"

"Girls, boys," Z said.

"Not choosy," I said. "And great natural charm."

"They wanna fuck a star," Z said.

"Dawn like that?" I said.

"Ready to play any game Jumbo wanted."

"He play games?" I said.

"Kinky stuff?"

"Yes."

"Whadda you think?" Z said.

"I'd rather not think about it," I said.

"He used to carry sex tools in a gym bag," Z said.

"Was Dawn Lopata his standard MO?"

"Sure. Had them scheduled, like regular. Days ahead."

"Any trouble before?" I said.

"Not much," Z said. "Couple pregnancies. Paid them off."

"And the boys?" I said.

"None of them get pregnant."

"The press?"

"They write about him, his lawyers go after them hard, and they get sort of discouraged. But what does get printed is Jumbo pretending."

"The public seems less willing to buy this kid's death," I said.

"Which means Jumbo is in trouble," Z said. "You flounder, they let you drown."

"So what is Jumbo Nelson really like?" I said.

Z shook his head.

"Sick," Z said. "Mean."

"I'da guessed that," I said.

Some clouds had drifted in front of the sun, and a light rain began to fall as we walked back to my car. Harvard probably had a deal with nature to clean up after someone barfs.

RITA AND I SAT with Jumbo Nelson in Rita's office. Jumbo's
agent was with him, and a new bodyguard he'd imported from
Los Angeles, who was wearing a black shirt, a black tie, and a
snap-brim hat.

The bodyguard leaned on the wall beside the door and folded
his arms. The agent was a good-looking woman in a cream-
colored pantsuit. She wore rimless glasses with a pink tint.

"I'm Alice DeLauria," she said. "I'm Jumbo's agent."

Rita introduced herself and me.

"Boston is quite lovely in the spring," Alice said. "I hadn't
realized."

"Can the fucking schmooze, Alice," Jumbo said. "Tell 'em
why we're here."

Alice smiled.

"Isn't he cranky," she said. "But okay, bottom line, we wish to discuss a change."

"Such as?" Rita said.

"Such as getting rid of this asshole," Jumbo said, and jerked his head at me.

I looked at Rita.

"Asshole?" I said.

She smiled.

"I guess he knows you better than I thought," she said.

"I would advise you strongly against getting rid of Mr. Spenser," Rita said. "He is very good at this work."

"He hasn't done a fucking thing to get this cockamamie charge off my back."

"If it can be gotten off," Rita said, "we will do it."

"I'm firing him," Jumbo said.

"You can't fire him," Rita said. "He works for me."

"Then I'm firing you," Jumbo said.

"You can't fire me, either," Rita said. "Because I quit."

"Quit?" Jumbo said. "You can't quit on me."

"Can too," Rita said.

"Well, fuck you, then. There's a few other lawyers around," Jumbo said.

"There are," Rita said. "And if you hire one, I'll bring him up to speed with where I am. Meanwhile, this meeting is over. Beat it."

"Alice," Jumbo said. "Goddamn it. . . ."

"Oh, shut up, Jumbo," Alice said.

She stood up and put her hand out to Rita.

"Well," she said. "Kind of short, but certainly sweet."

Rita smiled and shook her hand.

"Kind of sweet," Rita said.

Jumbo stood up.

"Fuck both of you," he said.

Rita smiled.

"Beautifully put," she said.

The bodyguard opened the door. Jumbo waddled through it at full speed, with Alice DeLauria behind him. The bodyguard went out after them and closed the door.

Rita and I looked at each other.

"Who you suppose does the bodyguard's wardrobe?" I said.

"George Raft," Rita said.

PEARL, SUSAN, AND I were sitting on the top step of her front porch on the first warm evening of spring. It was still light. The sun wouldn't set until after seven o'clock. Susan and I were having cocktails. Pearl was surveying Linnaean Street.

"You're going to stay with the case even though you're fired," Susan said.

"You think?" I said.

She smiled.

"I know," she said.

"Why would I do that?" I said.

"Because you told Martin Quirk that you would," Susan said.

"I didn't say I'd do it for free."

"But you will if you have to," she said.

"How can you be so sure?" I said.

"Because you are a simple tool, and I know you better than I know anything."

"Don't be so cocky," I said. "You might be wrong, sometimes."

"Are you sticking with the case?"

"Well," I said, "yeah."

"Is it because you told Quirk you'd do it?" Susan said.

"Well, yeah."

"Is anybody paying you?"

"Well, no."

"See?"

"Okay, you got that part right," I said. "But it doesn't make me a simple tool."

"I could sum you up in a sentence," Susan said.

"What would it be?"

"You do what you say you'll do. You aren't afraid of much. And you love me."

"That's three sentences," I said.

"I separated them by semicolons," Susan said.

Sitting between us, as was her wont, Pearl was staring intently at a squirrel across the street. The yard was fenced and the gate was closed, so there wasn't much else she could do, but she was giving it a hell of a stare. We sipped our drinks. People passed. Several smiled at the three of us. Susan spoke to some of them.

"Would you ever put your underpants on backward?" I said.

"Is this a trick question?" Susan said.

"No," I said. "Dawn Lopata's underpants were on backward when they took her to the hospital."

Susan shook her head.

"No one would make that mistake," she said.

"Unless it was a man and he was rushed," I said.

"Unless that," Susan said.

"Also," I said, "she had rather large breasts but no bra."

"How large?"

"I never saw her in person," I said, "but in pictures she seems in the D-cup range."

"Did she seem to be braless in the pictures?" Susan said.

"No."

"It's not a dilemma I've ever faced," Susan said. "But most women would not want to go braless with breasts that big."

"My thought exactly."

"And you are wondering if maybe someone else dressed her?" Susan said. "And getting the bra on was too much work?"

"I am."

"Would that mean that Jumbo did it?"

"Nope. But it means somebody wanted to, ah, clean up the scene a little."

"Z?" Susan said.

"Probably."

"Have you consulted Quirk about this?" Susan said.

"No."

"Don't you think you ought to?" Susan said.

"No."

"Why not?" she said. "Why not take advantage of what he might have learned already?"

"We decided not to consult," I said.

"Why not?"

"We both think the best thing is for me to start from scratch," I said. "And reach a conclusion and compare it with Quirk's."

"He said that?"

"No."

"So . . . ?"

"I mentioned it, and he agreed. There's stuff you know," I said, "without saying much."

"Oh," Susan said. "I'm blundering into that male thing again."

"No matter where you go," I said, "you don't blunder."

"Thank you," Susan said. "But talk to me about the, ah, male thing, a little more."

"Quirk wants to know if Jumbo's guilty. He doesn't care if he can prove it. But he wants to know. If I go through the exercise and conclude that Jumbo is guilty, and Quirk's conclusion is the same, then he can relax and let them railroad Jumbo, even if there's no proof."

"And that's justice?" Susan said.

"Enough justice for Quirk," I said. "As long as he's sure Jumbo is guilty."

"But he's never said all this."

"Mostly not," I said.

"But you know it," Susan said.

"I do."

"Because that would be enough justice for you," she said.

"It would," I said.

The squirrel had vanished, and Pearl was now staring thoughtfully into the middle distance.

"And if you conclude that Jumbo didn't do it, or at least didn't do it with intent . . . ?"

"I'll report it to Quirk, and he'll have to decide."

"If he decides to fight it?" Susan said.

"I'll help him."

"If he decides to let Jumbo be railroaded?" Susan said.

"He won't," I said.

All three of us sat for a bit, looking into the middle distance.

Then I said, "May I mix us up some fresh drinks?"

"Yes," Susan said. "You may."

So I did.

Zebulon Sixkill VI

"A bouncer?" Lucy said. "I can't be with a bouncer, for God's sake."

"Gotta make a living," Zebulon said.

"How much living can a bouncer make?" Lucy said.

"Don't know."

"You didn't even ask?"

"No."

"What's wrong with you?" she said.

"Don't know," Zebulon said.

"You're not going to play football anymore?"

"Guess not."

Lucy stared at him silently, and as she stared, he could almost see her withdraw into the perfect gloss of herself.

"Thank God we didn't get married," she said.

"Why?"

"It would have been so much harder to leave you," she said.

"Leave?"

"My family disapproves of divorce," she said.

"You're going to leave?"

"One minute I'm living in a nice condo with the campus God, the man who's going to be a famous professional player and make millions of dollars."

Zebulon shrugged.

"Next minute I'm living in some dump with an Indian from Montana who works as a bouncer?"

"I guess," Zebulon said.

"I wasn't brought up for that, Z. I can't be that."

"Maybe I can get back in shape," Zebulon said. "Transfer. Take care of business."

"Maybe," Lucy said. "Maybe. Maybe. I can't wait for that, Z. The girls in my sorority used to call me Sister Squaw. They were jealous. Now they won't call me that.

But they'll laugh behind my back. Last year's homecoming queen. This year's joke."

"You don't love me," Zebulon said.

Lucy looked at him silently for a moment. She seemed as if she might cry. But she didn't.

Instead, she said, "Not enough."

I WAS WITH Z. We were confronting the heavy bag in Henry Cimoli's boxing room. Both of us wore light speed-bag gloves.

"You're hitting it with your arms," I said.

He was stripped to the waist, the sweat glistening on his body.

"You get your power from your legs," I said, "and from your stomach and waist. Watch me. . . . You keep him off you with a left jab, say."

I demonstrated.

"Then, I'm exaggerating the movement and slowing it down so you can see it . . . In a crouch, like so, feet solid under you, and you lead with your right hip a little, that twists your body a little at the waist, and you torque the right cross around behind the hip, as your body unwinds, and all of you, once you got it mastered, explodes into the punch."

I hit the bag, very hard. Z nodded.

"If I can remember," he said.

"You don't remember," I said. "You do it until it becomes muscle memory. Like riding a bicycle."

"Crees don't ride bicycles," he said, and went into his boxing stance. He put a sharp jab on the bag that made it jump, then led a bit too much with his right hip and delivered a right cross, hard into the heavy bag.

"Good," I said. "Coupla thousand more reps, it'll be as natural as breathing."

"Almost there," Z said, and hit the bag again.

"Gimme ten more," I said.

Which he did. When he stopped, he was puffing but not a lot. I nodded at the stool near the ring, and Z went and sat.

"You doing your intervals?" I said.

"Four times a week," he said.

"How's that going?"

"I'm up to fifteen intervals," he said.

"We can do some intervals on the heavy bag, too," I said.

"Hit it fast and slow?" Z said.

"There's a couple of approaches," I said. "You been spending time with Henry?"

"Yeah."

"Can't hurt," I said.

"Not drinking much, either," Z said.

"No harm to that," I said.

DAWN'S FRIEND CHRISTINE gave me the names of several men who had dated Dawn. The first two I talked with said they'd been out with her only once. One of them said she was too needy. The other one said she was kind of boring. Neither seemed eager to be associated with a murder inquiry. The third dater's name was Marc Perry. I met him on a construction site, where he was working as a carpenter. He had dated her in high school, and he was more interesting.

"You been doing this since high school?" I said.

"Naw, went to Brown," he said.

"Graduate?" I said.

"BA in psych," he said. "Maybe I'll go to grad school in a

while, I don't know. At the moment, I'm sort of looking around, and while I'm looking around, I kind of like this work."

"Yeah," I said. "I would, too. Tell me about Dawn Lopata."

"That guy really kill her?" he said.

"Something did, don't know if it was him," I said.

"Too bad," he said. "She was an okay kid."

"You liked her?"

"Sure," Perry said.

"One of the other guys I talked with said she was needy," I said.

"Yeah," Perry said. "Yeah, I guess she probably was."

"How so?" I said.

"You know, she was always afraid she didn't measure up. Like she always seemed worried that you were just there to bang her."

"She was sexually available?"

"Aren't they all."

"I've always hoped so," I said. "Passive or aggressive?"

"Hey," he said. "Were you a psych major, too?"

"I'm best friends with one," I said. "Was she one of those women who sort of submit, or did she seek?"

"Funny thing is," he said, "she was both. She seemed eager, and she was very interested in whatever sexual contrivance you could, ah, come up with."

"Positions?" I said. "Sex aids?"

"Yeah, whatever you might know that she hadn't tried."

"And the passive part?" I said.

"Once you were, like, in the saddle, or whatever, she just lay there."

"No response?"

"Limp as a glove," he said.

"She ever play choking games?"

"Like cut off her breathing so she gets an extra thrill?"

"Yeah," I said.

"I got no interest in that stuff," he said. "Wouldn't do it if I was asked."

"She ask?" I said.

"Nope. You think that's how she got killed?"

"Don't know," I said. "Why I'm asking."

"I read that he strangled her," Perry said.

"Me too," I said.

"But you don't know."

"Why I'm asking," I said. "Any of the other guys that dated her play choking games, that you know about?"

"No," Perry said. "But it's not the kind of thing most guys talk about."

"The sex that she was interested in, was that primarily aimed at intensifying your experience or hers?"

He was silent for a time.

"I don't know," he said. "You know? I mean, you're doing something that really turns the girl on, it usually turns you on, too, doesn't it. I assume that would be vice versa with her. I can't believe I'm talking about shit like this with a stranger."

"Lucky. You were a psych major," I said.

"Doesn't seem to be doing me much good at the moment," he said.

"Any theories about why she was the way she was?" I said.

He grinned.

"Failure to resolve the conflict between passivity and aggression," he said.

"Ah," I said. "That clears it up."

"A BA in psych don't make me a shrink."

"I know," I said. "But it might help you pay attention."

He nodded.

"All I can give you," he said, "is how she was really worried that you cared about her for herself, not for the sex."

"Did you?"

"I liked her okay," Perry said.

"With or without sex?"

"Sure," he said.

He looked down, and while he was looking down, he adjusted the hammer in his hammer holster.

"Honestly?" he said.

"I'd prefer it," I said.

"She wasn't the brightest bulb in the chandelier," he said.

"Uh-huh."

"I was nineteen," he said.

"Uh-huh."

"Oh, hell," he said. "Course not. She wasn't coming across, I wouldn'ta dated her."

I nodded.

"So her fears were well founded," I said.

"Yeah," he said.

"And most of the people she dated felt that way?"

"Yeah."

He shook his head.

"She was kind of a joke," he said.

I nodded. We were quiet. Perry absently jiggled the hammer in its holster.

"I feel kind of bad for her," he said.

"Me too," I said.

"And I feel kind of bad about myself and how I was with her."

"Probably should," I said. "On the other hand, nineteen and male is nineteen and male."

"I know that, too," Perry said.

IT WAS RAINY again this April. I worked out at the Harbor Health Club, and when I got through I went into Henry Cimoli's office and drank some coffee with him, and watched the gray rain make circular patterns on the gray ocean through Henry's big picture window.

"Got some donuts," Henry said. "Cinnamon. Want one?"

"How many you got," I said.

Henry opened the bottom drawer of his desk and took out a box and looked in.

"Ten," he said.

"You're not having any?" I said.

"I was hoping we could share," Henry said.

I took a donut.

"Like the view?" Henry said.

"Better than the blank wall that used to be there," I said. "With the torn boxing poster of you."

Henry grinned and leaned back and put his feet up on his desk. His sneakers were silver and black. He was wearing white sweats and a white sleeveless jacket with the collar turned up, and a gold chain around his neck.

"Bought this place 'cause it was a dump and it was cheap, and the clientele I was serving were guys like you and Hawk, and you wasn't afraid to come down to the waterfront to work out," Henry said. "People think I am really smart to have jumped in ahead of the next big real estate trend."

"You had no idea," I said.

"None," he said. "And about five years after I bought the place, the waterfront went sky-high fucking yuppie."

"As did you," I said.

"You like my outfit?" he said.

"You look like a very short Elvis impersonator," I said.

"Hey, it's a costume. I put one like it on every day. We don't have spit buckets in the corners anymore. Health-club business is aimed at women. They think it's adorable to belong to a swishy club on the waterfront run by an actual live former boxer."

He grinned and flexed his arms.

"With visible biceps," he said.

"Cute," I said.

"Why I like Z working out here. He looks like every house-wife's dream: dark, big, muscular, sort of dangerous. Hot damn," Henry said. "An orgasm waiting to happen. Some of them would jump him in the boxing room if they wasn't afraid I'd yank their membership."

"Which you wouldn't," I said.

"Course I wouldn't."

"Z says you been working with him," I said.

"Since he moved in here," Henry said.

"How's that going?" I said.

"Fine. I got a couple rooms here I keep, case I need to stay late, or whatever."

"You're too old for whatever," I said.

"Depends how often whatever comes my way," Henry said. "Lately I've been trying to cut back to one a day."

"Successfully, I'll bet."

"Sure," Henry said. "Anyway, Z's got a lot of potential. And it looks cool to the ladies for me to be boxing with the Big O."

"I like his potential, too," I said.

"He's quick," Henry said. "He's very strong. And he's a real good athlete, you know? He picks everything up quick. Got a woman here, teaches martial arts, she's been showing him a few moves. He doesn't mind learning from a woman. He gets it at once, and . . . he's amazing."

"And he's tough," I said.

"Absolutely. He'll work himself until he gets sick."

"He wants it," I said.

"Whatever *it* is," Henry said.

I picked up another donut.

"You know what it is," I said. "You used to want it, too."
Henry smiled.

"I got it," he said. "He juiced?"

"He was," I said.

"Has the look," Henry said. "He needs to get off them."

"I'll make the suggestion," I said.

Zebulon Sixkill VII

The club was in Hollywood, and the haul back and forth from Garden Grove was long. So when his month of grace ran out, Z got a one-room apartment on Franklin Avenue, from which he could walk to work.

The club had a fancy front façade with a scary-looking black guy named Deevo working the door. He had a Mohawk, and a scar on his jawline. Z worked inside, where there was a long bar, a lot of waitresses in short skirts, and a small stage upon which nude women danced and did stand-up comedy. The crowd was largely male. But there were always some couples there that got heated up by the naked performers. Many of the people who came were regulars, including a famous movie comedian named Jumbo Nelson, who was there several nights a week, usually with young women, and a tall bodyguard in a black suit who used to lean on the bar near Z and watch Jumbo.

Z had been working the club for six months when, on a crowded Friday night, with a heavy rain coming down outside, Jumbo Nelson slid his hand up the dress of a dark-haired woman sitting at the next table with a male companion.

"Hey," the woman said, and slapped at his hand. "You see what he done, Ray?"

"I seen," Ray said.

He stood and walked to Jumbo and grabbed him by the collar. Z started over, but the bodyguard got there first.

The bodyguard said, "Ease off, pal."

Ray picked up a beer bottle from Jumbo's table and swung it against the bodyguard's forehead. The bottle broke and the blood began to run down the bodyguard's face. Z arrived and gave Ray the same kind of forearm that he had used to ward off tacklers. It put Ray down. Deevo arrived, and he and Z got Ray on his feet and walked him out with the wronged woman behind them screaming that they wanted their fucking money back. Deevo stayed outside and put them in a cab. Z came back in and put a folded Kleenex over the cut on the bodyguard's face. He taped it in place.

The bodyguard said he'd get it stitched later, after he drove Jumbo home. Later, on his way out, Jumbo gave Deevo and Z each a one-hundred-dollar bill. He also gave Z a business card.

"I like your style, Tonto," Jumbo said. "Gimme a call, might hire you."

IT HAD RAINED fourteen out of the first nineteen days of this month. And it was at it again. I was in my office, reading *Doonesbury, Arlo & Janis,* and *Tank McNamara.* I spent a lot of time on *Doonesbury,* because I had to read it twice. When I finished, I poured some fresh coffee and began to think about Dawn Lopata.

That she had spent sexual time with Jumbo seemed certain. That during that time she had died also seemed certain. Who was responsible for that, and why, was not certain. After being at this for a month, I knew more about everybody involved. But I didn't know how Dawn Lopata died. I looked down through the rain at Berkeley Street, where there was a jangle of colorful umbrellas.

"Progress," I said to the street, "is our most important product."

My office door opened behind me. I swiveled around. And two men came in. Maybe progress had come knocking. The taller man was evenly tanned, with a big mustache and silvery hair worn long. He was wearing pressed jeans and black lizard-skin cowboy boots, with a black velvet blazer and a white shirt unbuttoned to his sternum. His partner was a little shorter. He was wearing a full Brad Pitt. Black shoes, black suit, white shirt, black tie. His tan was darker than the other guy's, and his black hair was slicked back tight against his scalp.

"Where's Moe?" I said.

"What?" the tall guy said.

I shook my head.

"A little Three Stooges humor," I said. "Pay it no mind."

I gestured the men toward my client chairs.

"My name's Silver," the tall guy said. "Elliot Silver. I run Silver Star Security."

He took a card and placed it on my desk where I could look at it.

"Wow," I said. "I feel safer already."

"This is Carson Ratoff," Silver said.

Ratoff put his card next to Silver's and sat down beside him.

"I'm an attorney," Ratoff said.

"Can't have too many of them," I said.

"We represent Jumbo Nelson," Ratoff said.

"Me too," I said.

"We would like to discuss that with you," Ratoff said.

"Let's," I said.

"Since local counsel, whom we employed, has been fired, and since you were employed by local counsel, why are you still investigating?"

"An unquenchable thirst for knowledge?" I said.

Ratoff looked at Silver. Silver nodded slowly.

"That must be it," he said.

"Sometimes I work for tips," I said.

Silver looked down for a moment and rubbed his forehead with the fingertips of his left hand. Then he looked up.

"So you don't have anybody paying you right now?" he said.

"Sadly . . . no."

"Maybe you could work for us," Silver said.

"Great," I said. "What do you want to hire me to do?"

"That depends," Silver said.

I smiled my friendly neighborhood gumshoe smile.

"On what?" I said.

I was pretty sure I knew.

"Lemme put it to you this way," he said. "You investigate your ass off, as far as it takes you, and you conclude that Jumbo is guilty as hell. Whaddya gonna do?"

"What would you like me to do?" I said.

"Tell us," Silver said.

"Happy to," I said.

"And nobody else," Silver said.

"Just the cops," I said. "Maybe the DA."

"And if you conclude he's innocent?" Silver said.

"I'll tell you at once," I said. "And the cops and the DA."

"Got no problem," Silver said. "But we'd like to see if there's something we could do about the guilty part."

"Like I tell you, and then shut up about it?"

"That'd be about right," Silver said.

"Our firm," Ratoff said, "pays consultants very well."

"That's what I'd be?" I said. "A consultant?"

"Yes."

"How much is my consulting fee?" I said.

"Six figures would not be unreasonable," Ratoff said.

"Wow," I said.

"There'd be a confidentiality agreement, of course," Ratoff said.

"Of course," I said.

"So you'll do it?" Ratoff said.

"No," I said.

Ratoff sat back and stared at me.

"Why?" he said.

"My dog would know," I said.

"Your dog?"

"Pearl," I said. "When she sniffed me, I would no longer smell like rain."

"Rain?" Ratoff said.

"What the fuck are you talking about," Silver said.

"Faulkner?" I said. "Surely you read *The Sound and the Fury?*"

"Never heard of it," Silver said.

"There's this guy, Benjy," I said, "who's retarded, and his sister Caddy always smells like rain to him. . . ."

"Shut up," Silver said.

I was quiet.

"We tried the easy way," Silver said. "It's not the only way."

"You could grovel," I said.

Silver shook his head.

"Don't fuck around with this," Silver said. "There's some very important people involved in this. L.A. people. You don't know them, and they like it that way. But trust me, they are important."

"To whom?" I said.

Ratoff took a try at it.

"There is a great deal of money invested not only in the current film," he said, "but in Jumbo Nelson."

I nodded.

"They are astute businessmen," Ratoff said. "They protect their investment. And their approach to protecting their investment is often quite direct."

"You work for them?" I said.

"I represent them upon occasion."

"Who are they?" I said.

"They prefer anonymity," Ratoff said.

"I'll bet they do," I said.

I looked at Silver.

"You?" I said.

"I am on retainer to Mr. Ratoff's firm," Silver said.

"My clients," Ratoff said, "consider you a loose cannon in this situation, and they want you out of it, whatever way is most efficacious, and they don't care what it requires."

"Efficacious," I said. "You sure you haven't read *The Sound and the Fury?*"

"I looked into you," Silver said. "Everybody said you thought you were tough and funny."

"But good-natured," I said.

"Well, I don't think you are either," Silver said.

"Not even funny?" I said. "That's cold."

"One way or another," Ratoff said, "this situation is going to evolve without you."

"Do your damnedest," I said. "Unless this was it."

"This was not it," Silver said.

"Good," I said. "'Cause this was pathetic."

Both men stood.

"You'll hear from us again," Silver said.

"Words to live by," I said. "Now get the hell out of my office."

Which they did.

26

Z AND I WENT a couple of rounds for the first time. Z did well. Even with the big, soft sixteen-ounce mittens, he rocked me a couple of times. When we were done he was breathing hard, but so was I. I was breathing normally a little before he was. But his recovery time was pretty good.

"You're a quick study," I said.

He grunted. It was hard to tell what the grunt meant, because the gloves had Velcro closures instead of laces, and Z was pulling on the closure strap with his teeth. I took it as "thanks."

We took a shower.

"Probably can ease off on the intervals today," I said as we were toweling off.

"No," he said. "Starting to feel in shape."

"Your wind is good," I said.

"Not good enough," he said.

I nodded.

"You know a guy named Elliot Silver?" I said.

Z shook his head.

"Nope."

"How about Carson Ratoff?"

"Nope."

"Anything unusual about the financing of Jumbo's picture?"

"I don't know," Z said. "Nobody told me."

"Window dressing," I said.

"What?"

"Part of his costume," I said. "I'm so important I have to have a bodyguard, and not just any bodyguard, I got one looks like Jim Thorpe, all-American."

"I'm lucky he didn't want me to wear a feather," Z said. "They making a threat?"

"Sounds like one," I said.

"It bother you?" Z said.

"I've been threatened before," I said.

"But you won't back off," Z said.

"Can't," I said. "I start backing off, and I'll be looking for another kind of work."

"What would you do instead of this?"

"Can't think of anything," I said.

"So you just don't allow it to bother you," Z said.

"That's about right," I said.

He nodded slowly.

"Maybe I should sort of hang around with you," he said.

"Backup?" I said.

"Sure," Z said.

"Can you shoot?"

"Hunted since I could walk," he said. "Five hundred yards, I can knock down a running antelope. It wasn't a sport for us. We were after meat."

"How about a handgun."

"Got one, never really used it," Z said. "I guess if you're close enough."

"You got a license in Massachusetts?"

"Yeah, production company got it for me, through the Film Bureau, I suppose. Somebody took me over for fingerprints and a picture."

"There's a range in Dorchester," I said. "We can go over there and shoot a little, part of the training program."

"So I'm in?" Z said. "Be like your bodyguard?"

"Give you an opportunity to emulate my sophistication," I said.

SUSAN AND I MET for supper at Scampo, which was located in the recently rehabbed building that had once been the Charles Street Jail.

"You must feel at home here," Susan said, looking around.

"Anywhere you are is home," I said.

"You silver-tongued devil," Susan said.

She ordered a martini. I asked for scotch and soda. The waitress went eagerly off to get it. While she was gone, I brought Susan up-to-date on the Jumbo Nelson affair.

"You think the threat is real?" Susan said.

"Probably," I said.

"And Z's going to—how do they say it on TV?—watch your back?"

"That's 'bout the size of it, little lady," I said.

"The Indian," Susan said.

"Yes," I said.

"Whom you are attempting to rescue?"

"Exactly," I said.

The waitress returned with our drinks, and told us about the specials and left us to decide. We touched glasses. I took a swallow. Susan took a sip.

"Well," she said. "He's not Hawk."

"No," I said.

"On the other hand, Hawk has had his whole life to perfect being Hawk," Susan said.

"True."

"Z's only had a little while."

"He may never be Hawk; no one else is, either. But he'll get to a place where he'll do."

"Unless the booze gets him," Susan said.

"Unless that," I said.

"How is his drinking?"

"Seems to have cut back," I said.

"You don't talk about it?"

"Not much."

Susan looked at me thoughtfully for a time. My drink was gone. Our waitress spotted that and came and asked if I would like another. I tried not to tear up.

"I would," I said.

"You still okay, ma'am?" the waitress said to Susan.

Susan said she was okay. Her glass was down a sixteenth of an inch, but it could have been evaporation.

"You're not trying to resolve his drinking, are you?" Susan said.

"No."

"You are trying to turn him into a man who can resolve it himself," she said.

"That's not quite the way I thought about it," I said. "But yeah. That's about it."

"And you think he's up to it?"

"In the long run," I said.

"But he's supposed to be watching your back in the short run," Susan said. "Can he?"

"We'll find that out," I said.

"It's not like you don't have people," Susan said. "Vinnie would walk around behind you as long as was needed."

"True," I said.

"And Tedy Sapp would come up from wherever he lives in Georgia."

I nodded.

"And Chollo, or Bobby Horse."

"I guess."

"Quirk, Belson, Lee Farrell?"

"When available," I said.

"But you choose a work in progress."

"People need to work," I said.

"For crissake, people need not to get shot, too," Susan said.

"Suze," I said. "I wasn't planning on having anybody watch my back. There's a time when I might, but not yet. I can't be who I am, and do what I do, if I'm calling out for backup every time somebody speaks harshly to me."

"I know," Susan said. "You are what you are and you do what you do. I accepted that about you a long time ago."

"So it gives Z a chance to see what he's learned and what he's about, without, at least not yet, too big a risk."

"I'd prefer no risk," Susan said.

"Me too," I said.

She shrugged and drank half her martini.

"And I accepted it all a long time ago," she said.

She picked up her menu.

"All the guys in all the world," she said, in what was maybe a Bogart impression, "I had to fall for you."

"Isn't it grand," I said.

She nodded as she looked at the menu.

"Yes, it is. . . ." she said. "Mostly."

I CALLED A MAN in Los Angeles named Victor del Rio, who ran most of the Latino rackets in Southern California. I had done his daughter a favor once. And he had done me a favor. And while we were on opposite sides of a lot of things, we were on speaking terms.

When you called del Rio, there was a protocol you had to go through. Bobby Horse answered the phone. I knew the faint Indian sound in his voice.

"Spenser," I said. "From Boston. I'm sure you remember me fondly."

"Whaddya want," Bobby Horse said.

"I'm working with a Cree Indian," I said.

"I'm Kiowa," Bobby Horse said. "I don't give a fuck about no Crees."

"Just reminding you of my Native American–friendly creds," I said.

"Yay," Bobby Horse said.

"I need to talk to Mr. del Rio," I said.

"Talk to Chollo," Bobby Horse said.

There was a pause. I heard Bobby Horse say something, and then Chollo came on the line.

"Who you need me to shoot today?" he said.

Chollo was a graceful, mid-sized Mexican who was probably the best shooter I'd ever seen. Vinnie Morris might be as good, hard to be sure, but if I had to bet, my money would be on Chollo. He had helped me out in a place called Proctor some years back, and more recently, he and Bobby Horse had helped me win a small war in a place called Pot Shot. As far as I could ever tell, Chollo wasn't afraid of anything at all.

"Nobody yet," I said. "I'm looking for information."

"*Sí.*"

"Guy named Elliot Silver, runs a security service out there."

"*Sí.*"

"Guy named Carson Ratoff, who's a lawyer."

"I know them," Chollo said.

"I'm working on the Jumbo Nelson case; you know about that?"

"*Sí.*"

"You ever hear the old Jack Benny routine?"

"About *sí*?" Chollo said, pronouncing it to rhyme with *high*.

140

"*Sí,*" I said, pronouncing it to rhyme with *tree.* "I'm told there's important money behind Jumbo, and if I discover that he's guilty, and say so, bad things will happen."

"For sure, to Jumbo," Chollo said.

"Know anything about important money invested in Jumbo?" I said.

"I'm a simple Mexican shooter," Chollo said. "High finance, you'll need to talk with Mr. del Rio."

"That's where I started," I said.

"Mr. del Rio likes me and Bobby to screen his calls," Chollo said.

"And I'm going to make it through?" I said.

"*Sí,*" Chollo said, and the line went silent.

I waited. It was probably two minutes before a new voice came on. It's a long time when you're on hold, but I had called before, and I knew the drill.

"Spenser? This is Victor del Rio," the voice said.

"Thanks for taking my call," I said.

"I don't forget things," del Rio said.

"Chollo tell you what I'm looking for?" I said.

"Of course."

"What can you tell me," I said.

"A great deal," del Rio said. "I am just ruminating on how much I will tell you."

"These people colleagues?" I said.

"Competitors, more precisely," del Rio said. "Not enemies, but they could become such."

"And you'd prefer they didn't."

"It will do me no economic good to make them such," del Rio said.

"For what it's worth, no one will know where I got my information," I said.

"Your word on that?"

"My word."

"Your word is good," del Rio said. "Allow me to think another moment, is there anything I could tell you that only I would know."

I waited.

Finally del Rio said, "There's two brothers, Alexander and Augustine Beauregard. They run a company called AABeau Film Partners, in Burbank. The company funds movies. Most people refer to them simply as Alex and Augie, and what they really do is they launder money."

"Mob money," I said.

"Yes. They are connected to many criminal enterprises here in the Southland."

"Mob wants to wash some ill-gotten gain," I said. "So they invest in AABeau Films. AABeau invests in movie production. When the film is made, take their cut, return the money to the Mob as profit from a legitimate enterprise."

"Loosely defined," del Rio said.

"Okay, you're not a film fan," I said. "But that's probably pretty much how it works, isn't it?"

"It is," del Rio said.

"And you know this because . . . ?"

"Despite my distaste, I have occasionally invested."

"Ill-gotten gain?" I said.

"No gain is ill gotten," del Rio said.

"I like a man who is clear on what he believes," I said.

"We both know what we believe," del Rio said. "The fact that we do not believe the same does not prevent mutual respect."

"No," I said. "It doesn't. Where do Silver and Ratoff come in?"

"Silver is AABeau's security consultant. Ratoff is AABeau's lawyer."

"They in-house?" I said. "Or do they have other clients."

"They have other clients, but it's probably camouflage."

"Same clients?" I said.

"As each other?"

"Yes."

"They seem always to work in tandem," del Rio said.

"Silver do detective work, or strictly security."

"He does some investigating, if needed. But mainly he supervises, ah, compliance, for AABeau."

"Strong arm?" I said.

"As required," del Rio said.

"And Ratoff?"

"Was a criminal lawyer," del Rio said. "Now he is a corporate counsel."

"Good lawyer?"

"Said to be very clever," del Rio said.

"Silver dangerous?" I said.

"They are all dangerous," del Rio said.

"Me too," I said.

"I know," del Rio said. "Chollo tells me you are as dangerous as anyone he knows."

"As dangerous as himself?"

Del Rio chuckled.

"Chollo cannot entertain the possibility that anyone is as dangerous as himself," del Rio said.

"I have that conceit, too," I said.

"I know," del Rio said.

"So if Jumbo gets busted for a crime like the one he's suspected of, a lot of people lose a lot of money."

"Jumbo is as bulletproof a cash cow as there is in the movie business," del Rio said.

"Despite being a world-class dildo," I said.

"Irrelevant," del Rio said. "Maybe even an asset to the adolescents who comprise most movie audiences."

"Ever see one of his movies?" I said.

"No," del Rio said.

"Me either," I said.

"There is a great deal of profitable business being done," del Rio said, "based on Jumbo Nelson. It is business done by a large number of people who have little regard for the well-being of anyone but themselves."

"Either he did it or he didn't," I said. "I'm going to find out which."

"If you live," del Rio said.

"That's always a consideration," I said.

"Chollo holds you in high regard," del Rio said. "If you don't live, he may choose to avenge you."

"Would that be good business?" I said.

"No."

"But you wouldn't prevent him?" I said.

"I do not believe I could," del Rio said. "And sometimes we do other things but business."

"So," I said. "Does this mean you, too, value me highly?"

"No," del Rio said. "It means I value Chollo."

HENRY CIMOLI WAS LEANING against the wall in the boxing room at Harbor Health Club, with his muscular little arms folded across his muscular little chest. I was beside him in my sweats. Z was doing intervals on the heavy bag. Hit it for twenty seconds. Rest for forty seconds. Do it again.

"How many of those you suppose he's going to do?" I said to Henry.

"I dunno," Henry said. "You know he's in here like four, five hours every day."

"What's he do?" I said.

"Combination on the heavy bag, practices the check-block move Harriet showed him, hits the speed bag."

"Harriet the martial-arts instructor?" I said.

Henry nodded.

"He jumps rope," he said. "Does his intervals, like now, on the body bag. Different interval times."

"Dedicated," I said.

"Well," Henry said. "He's living right here, got no money, nothing else to do."

"What a motivator," I said.

Henry shrugged.

"Business is tough, you gotta be able to motivate yourself."

Z stopped and walked over to us, breathing very hard.

"Can you talk?" I said.

"I . . . talk," Z answered. "Got . . . nothing . . . to say."

"When you are breathing again," I said. "I'll show you a new move."

"Any . . . time," Z said. "I . . . ready now."

I grinned.

"Sure you are," I said. "Just let me rest up a little."

"You . . . think you . . . need it," Z said.

"I do," I said. "While you're waiting for me to stabilize, why don't you sit on that stool."

Z sat.

I took my gun off my hip, opened the cylinder, and took out the bullets. I put the bullets in my pocket.

"Okay," I said. "It's unloaded. We'll play with it on this mat, so if it gets knocked loose and hits the floor, it won't get too banged up."

We waited. Z's breathing became calm. I glanced at the clock. Pretty quick recovery time. He had gotten himself in shape.

He stood.

"Okay," he said.

"Sometimes a guy has a gun," I said. "If he's smart, he stays out of reach with it. Stand five or six feet away and point a gun at me, and there's not much I can do, but come in close . . ."

I stepped close to Z and handed him the gun.

"Put it against my forehead," I said.

Z did as I said.

"Now," I said. "The minute I move, pull the trigger."

'Like I'm trying to kill you," Z said.

"Just like that."

"Okay," Z said.

I waited a moment, then suddenly thrust my left hand up under his gun arm, grabbing the wrist, and fully extended my arm.

Click!

"Where was the gun pointing," I said to Henry, "when it clicked."

"Straight at the ceiling," Henry said.

"Try again," Z said.

We did, and two more times.

Each time, Henry called "ceiling."

"What happened next?"

"Probably try to pull your windpipe out of your neck," I said. "We'll go through it slow. . . . See where my hand is on your wrist?"

We stopped and looked at it. Z nodded.

"Here's another reason not to get too close. Point the thing at me from a foot or two away, say chest level. Pull the trigger first move I make."

Z pointed the gun.

I made a crisscross motion with both hands, and the gun fell to the mat unclicked.

"Jesus Christ," Z said.

I picked up the gun and handed it to him.

"We'll go through it slow," I said. "Right hand comes in against the inside of the gun-hand wrist. Left hand comes from the other side and hits the back of the gun hand. It scissors the gun out, even if you know it's coming. Ready."

"Go," Z said.

I made my crisscross, and the gun hit the mat again.

"You need to assume you got nothing to lose," I said. "Before you use either maneuver."

"Nothing to lose all my life," Z said.

Zebulon Sixkill VIII

Z's time with Jumbo was a swamp of disjointed images.

Besides his movies, Jumbo had a weekly one-hour variety show that retroed to the fifties. The show went on air at eight p.m. Eastern time, out of Burbank, taped at four in the afternoon, Pacific time, in front of a live audience. Z would sit with Jumbo in the dressing room while Jumbo drank vodka on the rocks and studied for his opening stand-up. Then the orchestra intro started, and he'd open the door for Jumbo, and Jumbo, in one of the six custom-made tuxedos he owned, would go to the wings and wait for the announcer, Art Maynard, to say, "And now . . . Heeeeeeere comes Jumbo."

Jumbo did a stand-up routine. There were some sketches, some guest stars, a band, some dancers. While all this went on, Z used to watch from the wings. Late in the show, he'd wander out into the audience and marvel at the number of people who thought Jumbo was swell. He also marveled at how nice Jumbo seemed onstage. It was as if the official Jumbo took over during the taping. Rollicking, good-natured, self-deprecating, quick, witty, knowing, and grateful for their attention.

At the end of each performance, Jumbo walked to the very front of the stage, bow tie loosened, and gazed down at the audience. With the camera zoomed in for a close-up, he would say, "I love you all . . . each . . . and every . . . one of you." And he would hold the stance as the shot pulled back and widened. They'd freeze the shot. The credits would roll, and it was over for that week. Usually Jumbo would have picked out a woman in the audience, and as Z started down the center aisle toward the stage, Jumbo would point her out to him. As the audience began to leave, Z would give her Jumbo's card and tell her that Jumbo was dying to meet her. If she was dying to meet Jumbo, Z would take her

backstage. Sometimes they'd consummate their relation-
ship in the dressing room, while Z leaned on the wall out-
side to make sure no one entered. Sometimes the woman
would require more dignified circumstances and Z would
drive them to Jumbo's house, and sometimes late at night,
sometimes early in the morning, drive the woman home.

"I ain't spending the night with her," Jumbo said.
"I'll fuck anything. But I sleep alone."

Jumbo never solicited young men in public. But now
and then Z would have to get up in the night and drive
one somewhere, usually West Hollywood, or Silver Lake.

In the morning, before Jumbo got out of bed, the
houseboy would bring him a lowball glass of sherry
on the rocks. At breakfast he would have Irish coffee.
Usually before he went to the set, Jumbo would have a
couple of purple-colored pills. He called them Violets.

"Sets you up good," he said to Z. "Try a couple."

So Z did. And it did set him up good. At lunch they'd
have martinis first and wine with, and in mid-afternoon a
couple more Violets. Evenings were martinis and cham-
pagne and more Violets and whatever young people Z
had been able to collect for Jumbo during the day. Some-
times there were too many, and Jumbo shared some girls
with Z. Z had no interest in boys.

"Stupid," Jumbo told him. "Go both ways, doubles
your chances to score."

One night they were so overbooked that Z spent half the night with three teenage girls.

Better get them first, he thought. *'Fore Jumbo's been there.*

He didn't have much to do to protect Jumbo. Push away an occasional autograph hound. Block the shot of some paparazzi. Mostly he was Jumbo's driver, booze buddy, and pimp.

IF THE TREES weren't blooming, you'd think it was late November. It was slate-colored and cold, with a hard rain falling as usual, and some wind. I sat inside in my office with my chair swiveled around and my feet up on the windowsill, and looked at the weather. I had a legal-size yellow pad of blue-lined paper on my lap and a ballpoint pen in my hand, and while I watched the day unfold I tried my hand at thinking.

I had made a list of people I'd talked to during the course of the Jumbo business, and I was checking it to see if I might have missed something. I didn't do a lot of scientific clues. Since nearly all the crimes I looked into were done by humans, it followed that nearly all of the clues I ever came up with were human. Something someone said or did or didn't say or didn't do, or even how they acted when they did or didn't. Whenever I was stuck, that's what I did. I made a list on a long yellow pad, of everybody, however peripheral, that I had encountered during the investigation.

Someone came into my office, and I swiveled around to see who it was. It was Quirk, wearing a brown tweed cap and a tan raincoat.

"Donuts?" I said.

"Was hoping you'd have some," Quirk said.

He took off his hat and coat, and hung them on the rack beside the door.

"Settle for coffee," he said.

"You know where it is," I said.

He poured himself a cup and one for me, gave me mine, and sat down across the desk from me.

"Just stopped by to see how things were going with Jumbo Nelson. They tell me you got canned."

"Me and Rita both," I said. "Although technically she quit before he could fire her, I think. It's a little hard to say, and you have to give weight to the question of intent. Did he intend to fire her before she quit. Intent—"

"Jesus Christ," Quirk said. "Whaddya know?"

"I found out a lot," I said. "I may well bring some miscreant to justice before I'm through."

"Did Jumbo do it?" Quirk said.

"Haven't found that out yet," I said.

"You got any idea?" Quirk said.

"No."

"What miscreants are you planning to bring to justice?"

I told him what I'd learned from Mr. del Rio. Quirk listened, silently nodding occasionally.

"Excellent," he said. "You're gonna clean things up in L.A. Just what I was hoping for."

"It'll lead back to Jumbo," I said.

Quirk leaned back in his chair and stretched his legs out in front of him. He slowly clasped his hands and raised them to his chin and held the position for a bit. Then he took in a big breath.

"You're making a list," he said.

"Everybody I've encountered in the, ah, investigation," I said.

Quirk nodded, and put his hand out.

"I see it?" he said.

I handed him the list, and he looked at it for a while.

"Didn't Jumbo have an agent?" Quirk said.

"Yeah," I said. "Alice Something-or-other."

I reached into my middle drawer and found the card she'd given me.

"DeLauria," I said. "Alice DeLauria Inc., offices in Century City. She's not on my list?"

"Nope."

"You talked to her before?"

"Nope."

"But you remember her?" I said.

"I do," Quirk said.

"How come you did and I didn't?" I said.

"Police captain," Quirk said.

"Of course," I said.

Z AND I WERE on the Boston side of the river, early, running intervals on the floor of Harvard Stadium. A woman in tight black sweats and in-your-face red running shoes was running the stairs of the stadium.

Z was watching her.

"Good ass," Z said.

"Absolutely is," I said. "But before you get in too deep. It belongs to the girl of my dreams."

"Her?"

"Main squeeze," I said.

"That's Susan?"

"Uh-huh."

"Holy Christ!" Z said.

"My sentiments exactly," I said.

"Sorry," Z said.

"I often have the same reaction," I said.

We reached the end zone and turned and sprinted the hundred.

"That's really your girlfriend," Z said as we turned and started to walk back.

"Amazing, isn't it?"

"Did I hear she's a shrink?"

"Yep."

"From Harvard?"

"She has a Ph.D. from Harvard," I said.

"And she's with you?"

"Every chance she gets," I said.

"Why?" Z said.

"Love makes strange bedfellows," I said.

When she was through with the stadium stairs, Susan came down and joined us as we ran our last interval. She had no trouble keeping up. When we finished, we went to sit in the sun on the bottom row of stadium seats, and I introduced her to Z.

She put out her hand. He shook it carefully.

"How do you do, ma'am," Z said.

"Susan," she said.

"Yes, ma'am."

Susan looked at me.

"Is he always this polite?" she said.

"He's intimidated," I said.

"Poor Injun boy," he said. "Off the reservation."

"What kind of Indian are you?" Susan said.

"Cree," Z said.

"And where are Crees from?" Susan said.

"You mean before Paleface steal our land."

"Yes, that's what I meant," Susan said.

"Northern plains," Z said.

Susan looked at me.

"Susan's geography is pretty well limited to Harvard Square," I said to Z.

"Montana, Wyoming," Z said. "Saskatchewan, Alberta. Around there."

Susan smiled and nodded just as if she knew where those places were. I knew, and she knew I knew, that she didn't know which direction north was.

"Do you speak Cree?" Susan said.

Z rattled off an answer in Cree.

"Oh, good," Susan said. "I like that the language stays alive."

"Mother could speak," Z said.

"You were close to her?" Susan said.

"No," Z said.

"Either of your parents?" Susan said.

"Drunks," Z said.

"Would you prefer to be called a Native American?" Susan said.

"No," Z said. "We're not natives, no more than you. Just come here sooner from someplace else."

Susan nodded.

"My date, here, has promised me breakfast. Care to join us?"

"Breakfast?" Z said. "It's quarter of one."

"I never eat before I work out," Susan said. "It's a great diner in Watertown. Close."

"No, thank you, ma'am," Z said. "Ate breakfast already."

He stood.

"Nice meeting you," Z said.

"And you," Susan said.

Z turned and headed off across the stadium. We watched him go.

"My goodness," Susan said.

"Most I've ever heard him speak," I said. "Christ, he was even sort of humorous."

"Not only did he talk," Susan said. "He sounded rather like you."

"You think?"

"I do," she said.

"Who better?" I said.

"No one, if your goal is to be a wiseass."

I grinned at her.

"What better?" I said.

"He looks good," Susan said.

"And," I said, "he admired your tush."

"See, he's very nice."

"Every straight male alive admires your tush," I said. "Not all of them are nice."

"Well, it's a nice trait," Susan said. "Z seemed very ill at ease."

"Yes."

"Is he that way with all women, or just Harvard-educated Jewesses?" Susan said.

"I think it's because he isn't going to have sex with you," I said.

"Why not?" Susan said.

"Because you're with me," I said.

"Oh, good," Susan said. "I'd hate to think he didn't want to."

"The straight male populace of the known world wants to," I said.

"Are you saying he only knows how to relate to women if they are prospective sex partners?"

"Be my guess," I said.

"And men?"

"Prospective adversaries," I said.

"And you know this how?"

"Because I know stuff," I said.

"You're so certain," Susan said. "How come you're so certain?"

"In the barren days before I met you," I said, "I might have had a touch of that."

"I'm shocked," Susan said. "Shocked, I tell you."

"Let's go eat," I said.

I CALLED A COP I knew in L.A. named Samuelson.

"Calling to see how it's going with a Boston guy as chief," I said.

"Best cop I ever worked for," Samuelson said. "Whaddya want?"

"I'm calling to inquire as to your well-being, and you're giving me 'Whaddya want'?"

"Correct," Samuelson said.

"Ever make captain?" I said.

"Yes."

"Makes me proud," I said, "just to know you."

"Will you get to the favor you want me to do you," Samuelson said.

"You think I'd only call because I needed a favor?" I said.

"Correct."

"That's cynical," I said.

"You think being a cop for thirty years is going to make me idealistic?" Samuelson said.

"Didn't you join the force in order to protect and serve?" I said.

"Sanitation department wasn't hiring," Samuelson said. "Whaddya want?"

"I'm interested in finding out whatever I can about a woman named Alice DeLauria," I said. "Jumbo Nelson's agent."

"Has her own agency," Samuelson said. "Alice DeLauria Inc."

"Ah, you know her."

"Her old man is to the Anglo Mob in L.A. what your pal del Rio is to the Latino Mob."

"His name DeLauria?"

"No," Samuelson said. "His name is Nicky Fellscroft. She's married to one of his associates, guy named Stephano DeLauria."

"He a hood?"

"Stephano? You bet. He's Nicky's enforcer."

"Any good?" I said.

"World-class," Samuelson said.

"And Alice DeLauria?"

"Close family," Samuelson said.

"She's in the business."

"Sure is. We've never been able to get anything that'll stand in court."

"One reason being that no one will testify against DeLauria's wife," I said.

"Or Nicky's daughter," Samuelson said.

"So how come she works as an actors' agent?"

"How many actors you figure she represents," Samuelson said.

"One?" I said.

"Correct."

"Jumbo?" I said.

"Correct," Samuelson said.

"She's his keeper," I said.

"That's right."

"You know why?" I said.

"Mob money is invested in him."

"I know," I said. "Can you prove it?"

"No," Samuelson said.

"I can't prove it, either," I said.

"But you know about the Mob money," Samuelson said.

"They invest in Jumbo's films," I said. "Wash dirty money, and make a profit, too."

"And you know that how?"

"You're not my only friend in Los Angeles," I said.

"Lucky for you," Samuelson said. "You working the Jumbo Nelson thing in Boston."

"I am," I said.

"Who you working for?"

"I'm sort of pro bono at the moment," I said.

"He kill her?" Samuelson said.

"I don't know," I said. "Homicide commander in Boston has his doubts."

"I'll pay attention," Samuelson said. "Anything passes me, might be useful, I'll let you know."

"Back at you," I said.

"Good," Samuelson said. "Be nice to arrest somebody."

"Always is," I said.

THE BIG WINDOWS in Rita Fiore's top-floor corner office gave a grand overlook of everyone who worked at lower altitudes.

"Above it all," I said.

Rita smiled.

"And yet still a woman of the people," she said.

"I've heard that," I said.

"For an okay time, call Rita?"

"I read it somewhere," I said. "I want to talk with Jumbo Nelson alone."

"Most people don't," Rita said.

"I know," I said. "But I do. And I don't want to have to fight with his bodyguard, or outwit his agent, or work around his lawyer."

"And you want me to help with that?" Rita said.

"Yes," I said. "Do you think, despite your recent estrangement, that you could get Jumbo to come see you alone."

Rita began to smile.

"We both know how to get Jumbo here alone," she said.

"Could you stand it?"

"I believe I could," she said. "As long as I don't actually have to be alone with him."

"That would be your choice," I said.

"I'm friendly," Rita said. "But not desperate."

"Jumbo would be a good working definition," I said, "of desperate."

"Maybe hopeless," Rita said. "Can you fill me in?"

"Seems fair," I said. "Since you're prepared to sacrifice your virginity for me."

"*A,*" Rita said, "I am not letting Jumbo Nelson within ten feet of my virginity, and *B,* I sacrificed it long ago, for two piña coladas and a half-hour of fun in the backseat of a Buick."

"Girls gone wild," I said.

"And the tradition lives on," Rita said. "Fill me in."

I told her what I knew about Jumbo's Mob connections, about Silver and Ratoff, Alex and Augie, AABeau Film Partners, Alice DeLauria, Nicky Fellscroft, and Stephano DeLauria.

"Wow," Rita said.

"Yeah," I said.

"You've been a busy beaver. . . ." Rita paused and smiled. "If I may use the term."

"No one better qualified," I said.

"You know a lot," she said. "About this whole business."

"I do."

"And how is it helping your case?"

"Gives me more people to talk with," I said.

"And what does it tell you about Jumbo?" Rita said. "Did he? Or didn't he?"

"No idea," I said.

"So you're going to try and get him alone and sandbag him with all you know and hope it shakes something loose," Rita said.

"I am."

"Mind if I sit in?"

"No, maybe you can help," I said.

"Maybe," Rita said, and leaned forward and spoke into her intercom.

"Margie," she said. "Get me Jumbo Nelson on the phone, please."

Then she sat back and smiled.

"You expect to get him just like that?" I said.

"Watch," Rita said.

In about five minutes, Margie's voice over the intercom said, "Mr. Nelson on line one."

"Thanks, Margie," Rita said, and picked up.

"Jumbo," she said. "Thank you so much for taking my call."

She sounded like one of those women in an erectile dysfunction commercial.

"No, no, you're very sweet. . . . Listen, you know, you and

I got off to a terrible start, but dammit, I don't know why we can't be friends. . . ."

She giggled.

"Well, actually, yes, that is the kind of friendship I mean. . . . No, me either. . . . But you are one of the biggest stars in Hollywood. . . ."

She giggled again.

"Define *big* any way you want to," she said. "Really? . . . What I was thinking was maybe we could spend an afternoon together that I'd remember all my life, you know? My afternoon with Jumbo Nelson . . . right here in my office . . . We have all that's required, a large couch, a private bar, a private bath, a lock on the door. . . . No, I'm serious. How many chances are there to make love with a movie star. . . . Yes, a lot of people tell me that . . . Oh, wonderful," she said. "How soon . . . Oh, perfect. Time for me to take a shower and shake us some martinis . . . Yes . . . Come right to my office. My secretary will be expecting you. . . . Not to worry, she knows the score. . . . Wonderful, I can't wait . . . You, too."

She hung up and looked at me.

"Being a hot broad has its advantages," I said.

She spread her hands and gestured at the big office.

"How do you think I got here," she said.

"By being the best criminal litigator in the Commonwealth," I said.

"And beyond," Rita said, "but a tight skirt don't hoit."

"It certainly don't," I said.

"And it doesn't do any harm, either," Rita said, "if people think I might discard it easily."

"More easily maybe than you actually do," I said.

Rita smiled.

"I'm pretty easy," she said.

"We all use what we've got," I said.

"Like you don't? You know what you look like. You know perfectly well that half the women in the city would disrobe in a heartbeat if you simply glanced at them."

"Now you tell me," I said.

"I'll sit in on this if I may," Rita said.

"Glad to have you," I said.

"How you want to play the opening moments?" Rita said.

"Margie will let him in," I said. "You'll be sitting on the edge of your desk with your legs crossed."

"You like that," Rita said.

"I do," I said. "So will Jumbo. I'll be behind the open door, and when Margie closes it behind him, I'll step out and lean on it."

"And then?" Rita said.

"We'll improvise," I said.

IT WAS TWO O'CLOCK in the afternoon, and through Rita's
big windows the harbor looked a lot bluer than I knew it to be,
when Margie ushered Jumbo into the room and closed the door
behind him. Jumbo had a box of candy. Probably kept a store of
candy for occasions like this. He started into the room. Margie
closed the door, and I stepped behind him and stood with my
back against it. He looked at me.

"What the fuck?" he said.

"Ah, yes," I said. "The ultimate question."

Jumbo looked at Rita.

"What's he doing here?" Jumbo said.

"We want to talk," Rita said.

"You fucking got me down here to talk?" Jumbo said.

"I did," Rita said.

"You lying bitch," Jumbo said.

"Exactly," she said. "Sit down."

Jumbo looked at the door and me standing in front of it. He and I both knew he couldn't get past me.

"You fucking people are digging yourself a fucking hole you'll never get out of," he said.

"I'll agree," Rita said, "that there's a hole being dug."

"I'm telling you right now, you got no idea the trouble you're in," Jumbo said.

Rita nodded.

"Sit down," she said.

Her voice was imperative. No curing erectile dysfunction now. Maybe causing some. Jumbo sat. He held the box of candy in his lap. Rita stood and walked around her desk and sat.

"I'm not trying to put you in jail," I said. "I'm just trying to find out what happened to Dawn Lopata."

"You can talk to my fucking lawyer about that," Jumbo said.

"You know Zebulon Sixkill is working for me now," I said.

It wasn't quite true. Henry had given him a job at the Harbor Health Club, handing out towels and bottles of water and checking people in. A condition of his employment being that he wear a tight white T-shirt. So I lied. It was nothing compared to the whopper Rita had recently told.

"I don't care where he is or what he's doing," Jumbo said. "He's a freaking loser."

I nodded.

"I'm gonna give you a list of names," I said. "Whenever you hear a name you know, tell me."

"What, are we playing some fucking parlor game."

"Elliot Silver," I said.

Jumbo stared at me.

"Carson Ratoff," I said.

"Whatever game you're playing, pal," Jumbo said, "I'm not fucking playing."

"Alex and Augie," I said.

Jumbo clamped his mouth shut.

"AABeau Film Partners," I said.

Jumbo opened the box of candy in his lap and ate a chocolate.

"Alice DeLauria," I said. "Your agent."

Jumbo ate another chocolate.

"Nicky Fellscroft," I said. "Your agent's father."

Jumbo seemed absorbed with his candy.

"Stephano DeLauria," I said. "Your agent's husband."

Jumbo ate some more candy.

"You know any of those people?" I said.

"No."

"Now, Jumbo," I said. "Don't be an idiot. One of them is your agent. You know Alice DeLauria?"

"Yeah, sure," Jumbo said. "But I don't know none of those other fuckers."

"You have any idea what any of them do?"

Jumbo's face attempted what might have been a sly look.

"Alice DeLauria is an agent," he said.

I said, "Now we're cooking, Jumbo. How about her father?"

Jumbo shook his head and chewed on a caramel.

"What's Z doing for you?" Jumbo said.

"Z?" I said.

"You said he's working for you," Jumbo said. "He been telling you shit?"

Jumbo had gone through the top layer of chocolates in the box. He took the crinkly little sheet of divider paper out and dropped it on the floor.

"We talk," I said.

Jumbo ate a candy.

"Well, he's fulla shit," Jumbo said.

"Lot of that going around," I said.

"Well, it ain't coming from me. I don't know nothing 'bout any of those people, except Alice."

I nodded.

"So how come Silver and Ratoff came to my office and spoke on your behalf."

"I don't know," Jumbo said. "What'd they say."

"They told me, sort of, to buzz off," I said.

"Maybe you should listen to them," Jumbo said.

He was unconsciously feeling the chocolates, apparently counting how many were left.

"That hole you mentioned that Ms. Fiore and I might end up in?" I said.

"Yeah?"

He ate a candy. Probably caramel, because it took some chewing.

"Who's going to dig it?" I said.

"You're digging your own hole," Jumbo said.

"And who will push us into it?" I said. "And why?"

Jumbo shook his head.

"You'll find out," he said.

Rita had been watching quietly. Now she spoke.

"Jumbo," Rita said. "The point is, he will. You don't know him as I do. He'll find out what happened to Dawn Lopata. He'll find out why everyone he listed is so interested in you. Everything. Remember, we were originally hired to help you."

"I don't need no help."

"Lemme tell you why you might," I said.

Jumbo rolled his eyes and popped another chocolate.

"I ain't got all day," he said.

"Nicky Fellscroft in L.A. has a great deal of ill-gotten cash that he needs to launder," I said. "So he takes the cash and invests it in AABeau Film Partners, which is run by Alex and Augie Beauregard, and retains Carson Ratoff as counsel, and Elliott Silver as a security consultant. AABeau invests the money in your pictures. They always make money. They are an ongoing franchise, and you can be reasonably expected to continue the franchise for a number of years."

Jumbo looked sort of pleased that I recognized his value.

"I do okay," he said.

"All of which makes you valuable, as long as the franchise keeps its nose clean. So somebody, probably Nicky Fellscroft, decides to give you a keeper, and his daughter becomes your agent."

"She's a good agent," Jumbo said.

He ate the last piece of candy and dropped the box on the floor.

"Sure she is," I said. "She's got style, she seems smart, she's got her daddy's clout behind her, and Nicky trusts her."

"You my agent," Jumbo said, "that's all the clout you need."

"How's my theory of the case sound to you so far?" I said.

"It sounds like bullshit," Jumbo said.

"I have a lot of facts, and I've only been at this a month or so. This case keeps cooking, and the cops will be all over AABeau and all their investors. How long you think it'll be before Alex and Augie and Nicky and friends decide to, ah, sever all ties."

"Whaddya mean?" Jumbo said.

"You think they want the cops questioning you and re-questioning you? You think it won't be a very appealing option to have someone simply make you go away?"

"Away?"

"You know what Alice DeLauria's husband does?" I said.

"No, what?"

"He's an enforcer for his father-in-law," I said.

"What are you telling me?"

"They'll kill you," I said.

"Nicky ain't gonna kill me," Jumbo said. "You're the one he'll kill. Both of you, and anybody else needs to be killed.

He's not gonna kill me. Kill Jumbo Nelson? I make people laugh. I'm funny."

"You're not funny," I said. "You haven't said a funny thing since I met you. You must have a knack of saying funny things other people wrote, but you're not funny. They'll be able to find another fat man."

"I'm getting out of here," Jumbo said. "You try and stop me and I'll . . . I'll sue your ass."

He stood.

"I'm trying to help you," I said.

He was moving his vast self toward the door.

"What happened to Dawn Lopata?" I said.

"I'm outta here," he said.

"What happened to her, Jumbo? You don't tell me, I can't help you."

"You're as good as dead already," Jumbo said. "You can't help jack shit."

"What happened to her?" I said.

"I don't know," he said.

Jumbo's voice was shaky, and had gone up an octave.

"I don't fucking know!"

He reached the door. I let him go. When he was gone, I looked at Rita.

"Maybe he doesn't," I said.

SUSAN AND I WERE HAVING martinis in my living room, looking out over Marlborough Street at the blue evening.

"Your session with Jumbo doesn't sound very productive," Susan said.

"Hard to tell," I said. "I didn't learn much I didn't already know. But I might have scared him enough to make something else happen."

"You still haven't talked with Z about the death."

"No," I said. "Not yet."

We sat on the couch, with our feet up on the coffee table and our shoulders touching.

"But you will?" Susan said.

"Yes."

"When?"

"When it's time," I said.

"And how will you know when it's time?"

"I don't know," I said.

"Well," Susan said. "At least you have a plan."

"Jumbo said at the end that he didn't know what happened," I said.

"And you believe him?"

"Maybe," I said.

"Not a ringing endorsement," Susan said. "You're sure he was there?"

"Pretty sure," I said.

"So how would he not know?"

"Coulda passed out," I said.

"There was booze," Susan said.

"ME said she was drunk when she died."

Susan sipped her martini and wiggled her right foot a little.

"When you spoke a little while ago about maybe scaring Jumbo enough to make something else happen," she said. "Could you talk about that a little more?"

"He's involved with some very bad people," I said, "who have invested a lot of money in him. If they fear for their investment, they'll do something."

"Like what?" Susan said.

"I don't know," I said. "I'm hoping he'll worry about that enough to come to me, or Quirk, or Rita, and speak up."

"So far what the bad people have done is warn you off the case," Susan said.

"I know," I said.

Susan carefully fished one of the olives from her martini and took a bite of it. She chewed thoughtfully for a moment. She could make a martini olive last for several bites.

"Do you suppose," she said, "that if Jumbo reported to them that you were pressing him, they might intensify their warning to you?"

"They might," I said.

"But we're not scared of them, are we," Susan said.

"Only a little," I said.

We were quiet while she finished her olive.

"Do you wish I were a pediatrician?" I said. "Or a software specialist?"

"No," Susan said.

"No regrets about what I do?" I said.

"You do what you are," Susan said. "I love what you are."

"No fear?" I said.

She washed down the rest of her olive with a small sip of martini and put her head on my shoulder.

"Only a little," she said.

Z WAS ON THE COUCH with his feet up, reading a newspaper. I was at my desk, looking at the list of people to talk with about Jumbo Nelson, when one of them walked in.

Alice DeLauria looked great. Black dress, three-inch heels, diamonds, and a perfect tan. She kept her sunglasses on. She saw Z and glanced at him without interest, put her small black purse on the edge of my desk, and sat in one of my guest chairs.

"You know my associate," I said. "Mr. Sixkill."

"I used to," Alice DeLauria said.

Z shrugged and went back to his newspaper.

"Coffee's made," I said. "Would you care for some?"

"This is not a social call," she said.

"I'll take that as no," I said.

"You recently lured my client to an office, where you bullied him and prevented him from leaving," Alice said.

"I did," I said.

"You admit it?"

"I do," I said.

If she'd had facial surgery, it was good facial surgery. It was a very good-looking face, except there was nothing about it that indicated feelings. That might well have been no fault of the surgeon, if she had one.

"Our attorney has spoken to you already about harassing Mr. Nelson," she said.

She took her sunglasses off and put them on the desktop beside her purse. Uncovered, her eyes were smaller than I'd expected, and about the color of blue slate.

"That would be Ratoff?" I said.

"It would."

"I thought he represented AABeau Film Partners," I said.

"We often consult with him," Alice said.

"Well, tell him I'm harassing as fast as I can," I said.

Alice looked at me silently for a bit.

Then she said, "Listen, hotshot. Jumbo tells me you know who my father is."

"Yes, I do," I said.

"And my husband."

"Him, too," I said.

"Why do you think I'm Jumbo's agent?" she said.

"Because you love laughter and good times?" I said.

"Because Jumbo Nelson belongs to us," she said.

"How so," I said.

"We have too much invested in him," Alice said, "for it to be otherwise."

"Nicely put," I said.

"I went to Barnard," she said.

"The value of a good education," I said.

"Yes," she said. "Well spoken, well dressed, poised, and articulate," she said. "I am also Nicky Fellscroft's daughter, and Stephano DeLauria's wife."

"Which means?" I said.

"Which means if I need to cut off your balls," she said, "I'm quite willing, and I have the means."

"Are you flirting with me?" I said.

"You need to take me seriously," Alice said.

"I know," I said. "It's one of my greatest failings."

"Not taking things seriously?" she said.

"Yeah," I said. "I'm ashamed, but there it is."

Alice nodded slowly.

"You think," she said, "that I'm some L.A. chick with pretty good legs. . . ."

"Very good," I said.

"Thank you, but here's how it's going to go," Alice said. "I warn you to get as far away from Jumbo Nelson as you can, and stay there. If you don't take the warning, some people will come around and hurt you. If you still don't get the message, some people will come around and kill you."

"Oh," I said. "You're not flirting with me."

She looked at me steadily. There was very little in her small-ish eyes that seemed feminine—nor, for that matter, quite human.

"Will you give it up?" she said.

"No," I said.

Alice looked at Z.

"My advice to you, Injun Joe, is to stay out of this," she said.

Z didn't look up from his newspaper. Alice stood, picked up her purse, and put on her sunglasses.

"You'll be hearing from us, soon," she said, and walked out.

WE WERE QUIET, listening to the rain fall. The scent of her perfume lingered.

"Good-looking," Z said.

"Except for the eyes," I said.

"Eyes looked kind of hard and empty," Z said.

"They did," I said.

"Hard to imagine bopping her," Z said.

"Scary," I said.

"She look at me with those eyes," Z said, "might not be able to get it up, you know?"

"I bet I could do it," I said.

"Brave man," Z said.

"Intrepid," I said. "You in?"

"In," he said.

"Hard to plan something like this," I said. "Basically we go ahead and do what we do and assume if something comes up we can handle it."

"I stay by you," Z said.

"This isn't," I said, "something either of us can do drunk."

Z nodded.

I got up and went to the closet and unlocked it. I took a Colt Python revolver, in its holster, off the top shelf, and a box of .357 shells. I walked back and put the gun and the bullets on my desk.

"Same gun you've fired at the range," I said. "Six-inch barrel. Six rounds in the cylinder. As you may recall, it's not brain surgery. Aim for the middle of the mass. Squeeze the trigger."

Z frowned.

"Could you write that out for me?" he said.

"If I thought you could read," I said.

Z got up and put the gun on his belt.

"How come I don't get one of those fancy semiautos like they all have in the movies?" he said.

"Revolver's simpler," I said. "Fewer moving parts."

"What you got?" Z said.

"Thirty-eight," I said. "Two-inch barrel."

"How come you don't get something bigger."

"I got something bigger, but the .38 is lighter to carry, and up close it works fine," I said. "Generally I don't need to pick people off as they ride along the ridgeline."

Z nodded.

"The .357 is kinda heavy," he said.

"Especially when it's loaded," I said.

"Wouldn't want to wear it empty," Z said.

"Good thinking," I said.

"You think she's serious?" Z said.

"Yes."

"You think some people gonna try and pound on you?"

"Yes."

"So there might be some fighting," Z said.

"Might," I said.

Z nodded.

"Good," he said.

"WHY DON'T THEY just shoot you?" Susan said. "Soon as you became an annoyance?"

She was preparing Pearl's supper, which was mercifully the extent of her cooking, except on rare and vaporish occasions when she decided to make us a meal.

"Not sure," I said.

Susan spooned some boiled hamburger with broth over the Kibbles 'n Bits in Pearl's bowl. Pearl sat perfectly still, and watched her intently.

"How much do they know about you?" Susan said.

"I don't know."

"If they knew about you, they'd know that a lot of people would expend a lot of effort to find who did it."

"Including you?"

"Led by me," Susan said.

She put Pearl's food down on the floor and patted Pearl on the shoulder as Pearl began to eat.

"Certainly," she said, "Quirk and Belson would give it special attention. Healy, the FBI person."

"Epstein," I said.

"And when Hawk came back from central Asia, he'd put together his own posse, don't you think?"

"Might," I said.

"He'd get Vinnie Morris, the Mexican man from Los Angeles."

"Chollo," I said.

"Who might bring Bobby Horse."

"Probably would," I said.

"I'm sure Tedy Sapp would come up. And maybe even that black gangster, you know, the one with the huge bodyguard," Susan said.

"Tony Marcus." I said. "The huge bodyguard is Junior, the jittery little doped-out shooter is Ty-Bop. How come you can't remember people like Tony Marcus, and you remember Bobby Horse like he grew up with you."

"I don't know," Susan said.

Pearl had cleaned up her supper, and was sitting again, staring at Susan.

"How can you not know?" I said. "You have a Ph.D. from Harvard?"

"Well, I did read somewhere that by adulthood, we are so full of accumulated data that our brain has trouble sorting it."

"Oh," I said.

Susan reached into a polished chrome canister on her kitchen counter and came out with an odd-looking item, which she handed to Pearl. Pearl ate it.

"What was that?" I said.

"Duck and sweet potato," she said.

"Part of our supper?" I said.

"No," Susan said. "Our supper is being prepared as we speak by the lovely folks at Upper Crust Pizza. It will arrive at seven."

"Large?"

"Yes."

"Not broccoli or brussels sprouts on it."

"No, I've put health aside this one time," Susan said. "What do you think of my theory about why they haven't shot you?"

"They may know a lot. They may not," I said. "But what they do know is that the murder of someone connected to the Jumbo Nelson case would fully engage the local cops."

"So they'll kill you only if it is less dangerous than letting you live," Susan said.

"Probably," I said. "But their success is not a foregone conclusion, you know."

"I know," Susan said. "In fact, I can only bear the possibility if I am certain they'll fail."

"Everybody has so far," I said. "Besides, if I can believe Alice DeLauria, my immediate danger is only a savage beating."

"That's consoling," Susan said.

"I was hoping it would be," I said.

"And you're not afraid," Susan said.

"I am afraid," I said. "It's overhead, sort of. The price of doing business."

"And you're able to push past it."

"Yes," I said. "Otherwise I couldn't do what I do."

"And you do what you do because?"

I shrugged.

"I'm better at it than I am at anything else?"

Susan nodded.

"And you read *Le Morte d'Arthur* too early in life," she said.

"Yeah, that too, I guess."

"And, I suspect, if you didn't do what you do, you'd be someone else," Susan said.

"Maybe," I said.

"And you won't let fear make you into someone else."

"What if I said to you, 'I love what I do but I'm too scared to do it'?"

"I know," Susan said. "I know."

"Yes," I said. "You do."

"I wish Hawk were here," Susan said.

"He'll be back," I said.

"Unless he got killed over there," Susan said.

"Hawk doesn't get killed," I said.

"Oh," Susan said. "Like you."

"Exactly like me," I said.

Susan made me a big scotch and soda, and herself an unusually large martini.

"Will Z be all right?" she said.

"Yes," I said. "He might be quite good."

"And if he's not?" Susan said.

"At least he won't be quite bad," I said.

"Have you noticed," Susan said, "that he's beginning to talk like you?"

"Who better?" I said.

We drank our drinks on the couch. Pearl was too late to get in between us, so she sat on the other side of Susan. Susan finished her drink, which was unusual, and put the empty glass down on the coffee table. She put her head against my shoulder. We sat like that for a time, until she turned farther toward me and buried her face in my chest. I put my arm around her, until the pizza came.

Z AND I WERE DRIVING out Storrow Drive in the late afternoon on a bright, cool Tuesday, to do some intervals at Harvard Stadium, when I picked up the tail. It was a black Cadillac sedan, and it was discreetly changing position behind us from time to time, doubtless hoping to deceive me.

"Aha, Sixkill," I said. "The game's afoot."

"The Caddy behind us?" Z said.

I looked at him. He shrugged.

"Injun read sign," he said.

"Let's make sure," I said.

I turned off Storrow at the Mass Ave Bridge exit, and went across the river and turned left onto Memorial Drive. The Caddy came along behind, trying to look like it wasn't following. I went all the way to the place where the Charles does a big bend, and re-crossed the river onto Soldiers Field Road, and stayed to the right of the underpass, and turned right to Harvard Stadium. By now the Caddy had figured out that we'd made them, and just came along behind us with no further deception.

The gate was open, and I drove in and around the stadium and parked near an entrance.

"Gladiatorial combat," I said. "On the floor of Harvard Stadium. Is that cool or what?"

"Gladiatorial combat?" Z said. "You are one weird white eye."

We walked under the stands to the field.

"Well, see," I said. "It's got a kind of Roman Colosseum design to it."

We stood on the fifty-yard line and waited. Z's breathing was maybe a little fast, but it was steady. If there was tension in him, it was the tension of a drawn bow. He was focused on the entrance we'd come through.

"Two reminders," I said. "One, try to stay on your feet. Two, stay in close. Guy your size especially."

"Three," Z said. "Remember what I've learned."

"Let that flow," I said. "Don't think about it."

Four men came out of the entrance tunnel and onto the field.

"You've trained enough," I said. "It should come as needed. Like riding a bicycle."

One of the four men was squat, with big hands, longish black hair, and a fat neck.

"You Spenser?" he said to me.

"We gonna fight?" I said.

"Not for long," the squat man said.

He put out a hard left. I checked it with my right and stepped around it as I blocked it with my left. I slid my left hand down, caught his wrist, pulled it toward me, and drove my right forearm against his elbow. He grunted with pain. I drove my forearm into his elbow again, harder, and felt the elbow break. He screamed. Someone hit me in the back of the head. I spun and hit him with the side of my clenched left fist, and continued turning, into a right cross that put the second guy down. I glanced at Z in time to see him bob under a big right hand from a tall kid with a gelled Mohawk and a weight lifter's build. Z turned his right shoulder into the bodybuilder's chest and drove a right upper cut up into the bodybuilder's chin that looked like it might loosen the guy's head. Mohawk took a step back, and Z hit him with a left hook just as the fourth guy put an arm around Z's neck. Mohawk took two more steps backward and fell down. The fourth guy, too, was an obvious bodybuilder, with his head shaved for scariness. Z dropped his chin and turned his head, which prevented Baldy from getting his forearm on Z's windpipe. Then Z quite thoughtfully located Baldy's feet and stomped his right heel down hard on Baldy's toes. Discouraged, Baldy let go, and Z introduced a move we hadn't taught him. He grabbed the guy by the throat with his left hand, and by the crotch with his right, lifted him chest-high, and slammed him to the ground. He wasn't out, but he didn't get up. The guy I had put down with a right cross had gotten to his hands and knees, and, like me, was watching Z. He decided to stay down as well. Mohawk was out. And the squat guy with the broken elbow was hunched up in pain and not threatening anybody.

"You boys local?" I said.

"You broke my fucking arm," the squat man said.

"I know," I said. "Hospital right across the river got an emergency room. You guys local?"

Nobody spoke. I bent over the guy whom Z had body-slammed.

"Where you from?" I said.

He mumbled, "Charlestown."

I nodded.

"Who hired you?"

He looked at the squat man.

"Bull," he mumbled.

I nodded.

"Bull," I said. "You were the contractor on this. Who hired you?"

Bull shook his head.

"Soon as you tell me, we're outta here," I said. "And you can get to the hospital."

Bull shook his head.

"Or," I said, "I could break the other one."

Bull stood with his head down, trying to find a place that didn't hurt to put his left arm.

"Guy named Silver," he said.

"Hospital's right at the head of the Charles," I said. "You'll see it when you get out of the stadium. Go west on either side of the river."

Then I turned to Z and held up my hand; he gave me a high-five.

"What about our intervals?" he said.

"I think we've done them," I said.

Z AND I WENT to the bar in Grill 23 for a victory drink.

I had a Dewar's and soda. He had Maker's Mark on the rocks.

"You have learned well, grasshopper," I said.

Z nodded. I sipped my scotch. He looked at his bourbon.

"Where'd you get the bodyslam?" I said.

"Television," Z said. "WWF."

"I suggest you lose it," I said.

"Worked like a charm today," Z said.

"Did," I said. "But the guy was a little quicker, or knew a little more, he'd have had time and opportunity to get a firm hold on your windpipe."

"What instead?" Z said.

"Stay on top of him. 'Specially a guy as big and strong as you are. Bombard him with more than he can prevent."

Z nodded. I had a little more scotch.

"Makes sense," he said. "On the other hand, I hadn't been there, they'd have had your ass."

"If you hadn't been there," I said, "I wouldn't have gone into the stadium in the first place."

"So you trusted me," Z said.

"Yep."

Z hadn't taken a drink yet.

"And you'll trust me again," he said.

"Yep."

"You had other people you could have called on," Z said.

"Yep."

"Why me?"

"Why not you?" I said.

"How'd you know I could do what you taught me?"

"This was a way to find out," I said.

"Christ," Z said. "A test run?"

"Yeah."

"What if I'd tanked," Z said.

"I figured they'd hire some local stiffs," I said. "And just on size, strength, and enthusiasm, you could distract them while I did my stomp."

Z looked at me for a while, then picked up his bourbon and drank some. He put the glass down on the glistening mahogany bar and looked at it. I looked at it, too. It looked so good, the amber liquid, the translucent ice, the squat, clear glass.

"I don't want to give this up," Z said.

"Maybe you don't need to," I said.

"I drink a lot," Z said.

"Maybe you cut back," I said.

"Everybody says that won't work."

"Everybody is generally wrong," I said. "Not everybody has to go all or nothing."

"You know that?" Z said.

"I did it," I said.

"You cut back?"

"I went from too much to not too much."

"You ever get drunk?" he said.

"Now and then," I said. "Not often."

"What if I quit for a little while?" he said.

"You think you're an alcoholic?" I said.

"I don't think so," Z said. "How do you know?"

"Something about you controlling the drinking or the drinking controlling you," I said.

"So if I could quit?" Z said. "For a while."

"Worth trying," I said.

"Maybe I'd know," Z said.

"Maybe."

"So what if I lay off for a month and go back and after my first drink I'm right back into the booze?"

"Then you'll know more about yourself than you do now."

"And I'd have to quit for good," Z said.

"Maybe."

"Be like a test run," Z said.

"Uh-huh."

"Like today," Z said.

"Uh-huh."

"No way to know if you don't try it out," Z said.

"Sort of like the scientific method," I said.

"What's that," Z said.

"Form a hypothesis and test it," I said.

"A hypothesis."

"Yep."

Z picked up his bourbon and drank the rest of it. I looked at the colorful pattern of the booze bottles stacked behind the bar. I listened to the soft human sound of the half-full bar. I thought about the evenings alone, perhaps with Pearl asleep on the couch, when I would have a couple of drinks before supper and think about me and Susan and all that had happened and all that we had done. No matter how many moments I had like that, they were all intensely moving for me.

"I don't want to start today," Z said.

"You're not doing it for me," I said.

"Meaning?"

"You don't drink because I'm watching," I said. "Doesn't really count much."

"So you're saying I shouldn't start not drinking while you're watching."

"Start when you're alone," I said. "And remember, it may be temporary."

"A hypothesis," he said.

"That you're testing," I said.

"Like today," Z said again.

"Which worked out quite well," I said.

"I'll drink to that," he said.

"Me too," I said.

I signaled the bartender.

A YOUNG MAN who needed a haircut came into my office wearing a seersucker suit, a white shirt, a blue tie, and a woven straw snap-brim hat.

"Spenser," he said.

"I am he," I said.

"My name is Corky Corrigan," he said. "From the law offices of Morris Hardy."

He took a card from his shirt pocket and laid it on my desk.

"Wow," I said. "I've seen Morris's ads on television. He looks implacable."

"Right," Corrigan said. "We represent Thomas and Beatrice Lopata."

"You and Morris," I said.

"Yes," Corky said.

"Have you ever met Morris Hardy?" I said.

"Certainly," Corky said. "He spoke at one of our associate meetings."

"You work for Morris?" I said.

"We are associated," he said.

"And you do the case," I said. "And Morris looks implacable and takes a third of the fee."

Corky gave a little head shake, as if there was a bug on his nose.

"We are bringing a wrongful-death suit," he said, "against Jeremy Franklin Nelson in the death of Dawn Ellen Lopata."

"Good for you," I said.

"I know you've been investigating the case," he said. "And as we assemble our witness list, I thought it might be wise to see what you've learned."

"I've learned that I don't know what happened," I said.

"But you must have a slant on things," Corky said.

He had a little notebook resting on his thigh, and had his Bic pen poised to transcribe things.

"My slant is pretty much a combination of subjective impressions and hearsay," I said.

Corky nodded.

"Useful background," he said.

"It is," I said.

"So go ahead," Corky said with a smile. "Don't worry about hearsay, leave the legal stuff to me, just relax and tell me what you've found and what you suspect."

"Where'd you go to law school, Corky?" I said.

"Bradford School of Law," he said.

"In Haverhill," I said.

He nodded.

"And you graduated?"

"Three years ago."

"And passed the bar?"

"Last year," he said.

I nodded.

"Mum's the word," I said.

"Excuse me?" Corky said.

"I don't want to tell you what I've found and what I suspect," I said.

Corky seemed startled.

"Why not?" he said.

"Don't see anything in there for me," I said.

"Don't you care about justice?"

"I do," I said. "Also truth, and the American way. But I am not so sure about civil litigation."

"Are you asking to be paid?" Corky said.

"No."

"Then I don't understand," Corky said.

"I'm sure you don't," I said. "I am still working on the case, and I don't want you, or even the implacable Morris, stepping on leads and tripping over suspects while I'm trying to work."

"Who is your client?" Corky asked.

"Nope," I said.

"Well, who do you recommend I talk with?" he said.

"Captain Martin Quirk," I said. "Boston Police Department. He's in charge of the case."

Corky wrote it down.

"Do you think he'll cooperate?" Corky said.

"Serve and protect," I said. "But it would be good not to annoy him."

"Do I annoy you?" Corky said.

"Let me count the ways," I said.

I WAS DRINKING BEER from the bottle, and Susan had a plastic glass of pinot grigio. We were sitting on the deck of the Institute of Contemporary Art in South Boston. Generally I found the art at the Institute somewhat too contemporary for me. I was more a Hudson River School guy. But the view of the Boston waterfront along the curve of the harbor was peerless. And in nice weather, we both liked to sit there and look at it.

"Wouldn't it be wiser for the Lopatas to wait?" Susan said. "I should think it would make their case stronger if he were convicted in criminal court."

"One would think," I said.

A big glassy excursion boat full of people drunk in the

mid-afternoon cruised past us, heading for a tour of the harbor and islands.

"And maybe they wouldn't need to sue," Susan said.

"If they were after revenge," I said.

Susan sipped a small amount of white wine.

"Yes," Susan said. "If the criminal trial seemed to be a miscarriage of justice, then you could bring civil suit, try for some justice."

"Seems so," I said.

"But if you wanted money . . ." Susan said.

"Then maybe you'd get right to it," I said. "Greed being what it is."

"It seems to argue that justice is not the motivation," Susan said.

"Does," I said. "Of course, human motivation is generally more than one thing."

"How do you know that?"

"Close observation of the human condition," I said.

"Uh-huh?"

"And you told me," I said.

"Uh-huh."

Some gulls sat alertly on the pilings, watching people eat. Occasionally, for no apparent reason, one would suddenly unfold his wings and sweep into the air. Then he would fly off, and return. Of course, since gulls look very much alike, I couldn't say for sure if it was the same gull.

"Do you think they can win?" Susan said.

"Not with Corky Corrigan running their suit," I said.

"Not even if Morris Hardy steps in?" Susan said.

"Morris Hardy will step in to take his third of the fee, if Corky manages to win," I said.

"Maybe Jumbo's people will settle."

"Probably," I said. "Which is what probably attracted Morris Hardy and his law offices in the first place."

"Because," Susan said, "he knows that Jumbo's people want all this to go away before the world finds out what Jumbo really is."

"Not calculus," I said.

"Can you do calculus?" Susan said.

"No."

"Do you actually know what calculus is?" Susan said.

"No."

"Me either," she said.

"And you a Harvard girl," I said.

"It's distasteful, isn't it?" Susan said.

"Calculus?" I said.

"That, too," she said. "But I meant the lawsuit."

"Distasteful," I said.

"Yes," Susan said. "I mean, I know it does the dead daughter no harm, and they might need the money, but . . . would you do it?"

"No."

"I'd do it to try and get even," Susan said. "For revenge. But for the money? No."

"Maybe they're doing it for revenge," I said. "Maybe they're trying to goose the criminal justice system."

"Or maybe it's the money," Susan said.

"Maybe."

We were quiet for a time, looking at the gulls and the boat traffic, and the cityscape across the water.

Susan said, "Something I keep meaning to ask you. It doesn't seem important, which is why I probably keep forgetting, but it's bothered me since you started talking about the case."

"Maybe you keep forgetting because you are lost in adoration of me," I said. "And it preoccupies you."

Susan nodded.

"That is often a problem," she said. "But in those moments when I can focus elsewhere . . . As you recall, I used to live in Smithfield."

"I believe it's where we met."

"Yes," she said. "Anyway, I always have wondered how she got from Smithfield to Boston."

"Dawn Lopata," I said.

"Yes."

I was silent for a moment.

Then I said, "Why do you ask?"

"Well, there's no public transportation in Smithfield. She'd have to drive. And if she drove, where's her car?"

"Maybe she went with friends," I said.

"The day she met Jumbo," Susan said, "wasn't she with college friends who live in Boston?"

"Yes."

"So?"

"Maybe they picked her up," I said.

"Maybe," Susan said. "Either of them own a car?"

"I don't know," I said.

"Another thing," Susan said, "that makes me wonder, is what I know about girls."

"You've had some experience at being one," I said.

"And treating many," Susan said. "I think if she were going to visit a movie star in his hotel room, she would go home first and shower and put on clean clothes as appropriate."

"You think?" I said.

"If nothing else," Susan said, "she'd want to shave her legs."

"Maybe she did all that in the morning, before she went to see the shoot," I said.

"On the off chance that one of the movie stars would invite her to his room for sex?" Susan said.

I shrugged.

"Ever hopeful?" I said.

"That could certainly be described as optimistic," Susan said.

"It could," I said.

"Probably nothing," Susan said. "But I'm curious. And I wanted to mention it."

"I'm curious, too," I said.

"Good," Susan said.

I had finished my beer.

"Shall I get us another drink?" I said.

"No," Susan said. "I think I need you to take me home, now."

"How come?" I said.

She smiled at me the way Eve must have smiled at Adam when she handed him the apple.

"I want to shave my legs," she said.

I CALLED THE SMITHFIELD POLICE and talked with a cop named Cataldo, with whom I had done some business years ago. He confirmed that there was no public transportation.

"Cabs?" I said.

"Not in town."

"Doesn't anyone want to leave?" I said.

"They drive," Cataldo said. "And good riddance."

"If you wanted to get into Boston and you didn't have a car, how would you get there?" I said.

"Why would I want to go to Boston?"

"See a ball game?" I said.

"That's why they make TVs," Cataldo said.

"Because you are a sophisticated urban guy?"

"Like you?"

"Not that sophisticated," I said. "How would you get here?"

"Borrow a car or get somebody to drive me."

"Thank you," I said. "If you never leave town, what do you do there?"

"Write parking tickets, keep the kids from loitering on the common, play softball, drink beer, bang the old lady."

"What else is there," I said.

"This about the kid got killed?" Cataldo said. "Dawn Lopata?"

"Yes," I said. "Know her?"

"Sure," Cataldo said. "Not a bad kid, really, just a fuckup. Always getting caught for something, like smoking dope in the girls' room at school, or cell-phoning nude pictures of herself that ended up on the Internet, or skipping school, or driving after-hours on a learner's permit. You know? Not evil, just fucked up."

"How about the family," I said.

"Old man's a blow," Cataldo said. "Big house, nice car, and no cash. You know the type?"

"Sure."

"Mother stays home mostly; she used to call a lot, see if we knew where her daughter was. Don't know much else about her."

"Older brother seems fine," I said.

"Yeah, good grades, played sports, went to Harvard," Cataldo said. "I don't know how he escaped."

"No trouble with the law," I said.

"Except for what I told about Dawn, none of them."

"You know what they got for cars?"

"Yeah, he just got a new one, and was blowing off to me about it."

"What kind?"

"Cadillac DTS, maroon."

"The big sedan?"

"Yeah, top of the line," Cataldo said.

"Anything else you know?"

"Lots," Cataldo said. "But not about the Lopata family."

After I hung up, I called Dawn's friend Christine. They had left Dawn after they lunched with Jumbo. Neither Christine nor James owned a car, and neither she nor James knew how Dawn traveled to Boston on the day of her death.

44

WE WERE DRIVING on Atlantic Ave.

"You doing any juice these days?" I said to Z.

"At Cal Wesleyan, we called them PES," Z said. "Performance-enhancing supplements."

"Still using?" I said.

Z shook his head.

"Not since Jumbo fired me," he said.

"What made you quit?" I said.

Z grinned.

"A great truth was revealed to me," Z said.

"Which was?"

"He was my supplier," Z said.

"How long you been doing them?" I said.

"Freshman year," Z said. "Playing, you know, like, major-league college football, you seem to need them to keep up. Guy you're competing with for the starting job is using. The pass rushers are using. The DBs on the other side are using."

"Who was your supplier then?"

"One of the alums," Z said. "Fella named Calhoun, was paying my way, he used to get them for me."

"Part of your scholarship," I said.

"Scholarship, hell," Z said. "I was on salary."

"Don't seem to need them," I said.

Z nodded.

"Always been a big, strong mofo since I was a papoose," he said.

"Papoose?" I said.

"Authentic Injun talk, Kemo Sabe," Z said.

"Christ," I said. "And I'm still learning to say 'Native American.'"

We pulled up in front of the Inn on the Wharf, where Dawn Lopata had died. The doorman came to the car. He was a sturdy young guy, and his nameplate said *Mike.* I gave him a twenty.

"Can we talk for a moment?" I said.

"Sure thing," Mike said.

"Name's Spenser; I'm working on the Dawn Lopata death," I said.

"Sure," Mike said. "Seen you here before."

"My associate, Mr. Sixkill," I said.

Mike nodded at Z.

"You remember her?" I said.

"The dead girl? Sure," Mike said. "I mean, she wasn't so special to remember when she came in, but then, you know, she gets killed, and everybody's talking about it and it's on the news and you go over it in your head . . . a lot."

"You remember when she arrived here?"

"I do," Mike said. "I was working early evening that week, and she came in a brand-new bright red Caddy. I mean, I'da remembered the car even if nothing happened. Leather interior, all the bells and whistles. Looked like it had about ten miles on it."

"She driving?" I said.

"No, a guy was driving. He let her off, and she went in the hotel, and he drove away."

"Remember the guy?"

Mike shrugged.

"Not much," he said. "Suburban-looking guy. Maybe fifty. I was mostly checking out the ride."

"Ever see her again?"

"I was off duty when the EMTs brought her out," Mike said. "But I hung around, so technically, I guess yes. But she was covered."

"How 'bout the car or the driver?"

Mike shook his head.

"No."

"You wouldn't have a number for the car?" I said.

"No, no reason," he said. "Maybe if we parked it . . ."

"He didn't come back to pick her up," I said.

"Not on my shift," Mike said.

"Thanks for your time," I said.

"Hope you catch him," Mike said.

"Hell," I said, "I don't even know who I'm after."

WHEN WE WENT IN to visit Buffy and Tom Lopata, Buffy eyed
Z silently as she showed us to the living room. She was wearing
tight black pants that narrowed to the ankle, black open-toed
sandals, and a black polo shirt hanging over the pants. Her
arms were pale and very thin. Tom joined us from upstairs, as
he had before. I wondered if they ever spent time together.

"My associate," I said to them, "Zebulon Sixkill."

Tom Lopata put out his hand. He was wearing madras shorts,
black penny loafers without socks, and a white shirt with a button-
down collar. His shirttails, too, were over his pants.

"Hi," he said. "How ya doin. Great to meet you."

Z shook hands and nodded.

Mrs. Lopata lit a cigarette.

"What the hell kind of name is Sixkill?" she said.

"Cree," Z said.

"What?" she said.

"Cree," Z said. "Indian tribe."

"You're an Indian?"

Z put up his hand, palm out.

"I come in peace," he said.

"So why is your name Sixkill?" Buffy said.

"Buffy," Tom said. "For crissake."

She ignored him. She was staring at Z.

"Goes good with Zebulon," Z said.

"Well, you are a strapping, handsome Indian," Buffy said.

"Yes," Z said.

"Could you folks tell me where you were the night Dawn died?" I said.

"My daughter?" Buffy said. "Is there a new development?"

"No," I said. "Not yet. I'm just trying to tie up some loose ends."

"Here, I suppose," Tom said. "Probably watching TV."

"That your memory, Mrs. Lopata?"

"We weren't watching together," she said. "He won't watch my programs."

"Hell, you won't watch mine, either," he said.

"I don't want to watch some dumb sports thing," she said.

"But you were both here, in the house, together that night."

"Absolutely," Tom said.

"No," Buffy said.

I looked at her.

"No?" I said.

"I was here, but he was out gallivanting in his new toy," Buffy said.

"Toy?" I said.

"She likes to joke," Tom said. "I got a new car; I may have taken it out for a spin, see how she handled."

"Red Cadillac sedan," I said. "Leather seats?"

"Yeah," Tom said.

"Nigger car," Buffy said. She snubbed out her cigarette and lit a new one. "Neighbors probably think he's a pimp."

Tom shook his head sadly.

"Doorman," I said, "at the Inn on the Wharf says Dawn was delivered to the hotel in a new red Cadillac convertible."

Tom stared at me.

"According to the doorman, the driver was a suburban-looking guy, maybe fifty," I said.

Tom didn't say anything. Buffy turned and stared at her husband. Z and I waited. Tom looked at Buffy.

"For God's sake," she said, "you are a pimp."

"Don't talk to me like that," he said.

"You delivered your daughter to that pig so he could fuck her to death," Buffy said.

"For God's sake," Tom said. "It's not like I knew."

"Pimp," Buffy said.

"She wanted a ride," Tom said. "I had the new car. Hell, she was going to have a date with a movie star, for crissake. Who wouldn't take her in?"

"Without telling her mother," Buffy said. "Either of you, without telling the mother."

"She made me promise," Tom said. "She knows what you think of her."

"Her own mother," Buffy said.

She put her second cigarette out carefully in the ashtray, picked up her cigarettes and a lighter from the table by her chair, stood, and walked out of the room.

"Shit," Tom said. "She'll go in her room and pull down the shades and turn on the TV. And she'll sit there and stare at it and chain-smoke for days."

"She do that when Dawn was bad?" I said.

"Any of us," he said. "Except maybe Matthew. She did it less with him."

I nodded.

"You dropped her and left?" I said.

"Yeah."

"Any arrangement to pick her up?"

"No."

"You dropped her and came home?" I said.

"Yes."

"Wife awake when you got here?" I said.

"No."

"You sleep together?"

He snorted a little humorless snort.

"No," he said. "Any way you mean it."

When we were driving back to Boston, Z said, "I've seen Lopata before."

"When?" I said.

"He was on the set, across from Jumbo's trailer, talking to one of the producers."

"He didn't seem to recognize you," I said.

"No," Z said. "I was in Jumbo's trailer, looking out the window."

"You know what they were talking about?"

"No clue," Z said.

"You were sober?" I said.

"Nope."

"But you remember this guy," I said.

"He was very . . ." Z waved his arms around. "You know?"

"Animated?" I said.

"Yeah, animated."

"You remember which producer?" I said.

"Sure," Z said.

"We can ask him," I said.

Z nodded. We were quiet for a time.

"You know," he said. "Neither one of them ever called the kid by name."

He'd grown more talkative recently, but quiet still seemed to be Z's natural condition. Conversation was always surprising.

"Seem too immersed in being mad at each other," I said.

"Why the hell do they stay married," Z said.

"You Indians just don't understand white-man ways," I said.

"Hell," Z said. "I'm still trying to figure out why you killed all our buffalo."

THE ALLEY THAT RUNS behind my office from Berkeley to
Arlington was named Providence Street. When Z and I came
down the back stairs of my office to get my car, which was
parked on Providence Street, I noticed that the Berkeley Street
end was blocked with a couple of orange traffic barrels. If people
have threatened to kill one, one becomes unusually observant. I
paused in the doorway.

"Odd," I said.

"The barriers?" Z said.

"Yeah. Usually there's a cop."

I looked up at the Arlington Street end. More barriers.

"Odder," I said.

"Street's one-way," Z said.

I nodded.

"Might be nothing," I said.

"Might not," Z said.

"Might be something," I said.

Z didn't say anything.

"Okay," I said. "I'll hang here. You go out the front door, turn right up to Arlington, and right again to that end of the alley. When I see you at that end, I'll step out."

"And?"

"And we'll see," I said.

Z turned and went up the three steps to the first floor and disappeared. I stayed where I was. Halfway up the alley was a white Ford van with tinted windows. If there was something, I was betting the van contained it. Ordinary-looking. Couldn't see in. Plenty of room for four or five guys and their weapons. Since the visit from Alice DeLauria, I had been wearing my S&W .40. I took it out and cocked it, and held it at my side. It took Z maybe ninety seconds to scoot around to the Arlington end of the alley. When I saw him, I stepped out of the doorway and began to walk toward him. He strolled toward me. The side doors of the van opened.

Bingo!

Four guys got out. None of them seemed to notice Z. One guy had a shotgun. I shot him in the chest. He stepped back, half turned, and fell with the shotgun underneath him. I ducked between two cars, and several bullets ripped into them. Z's .357 boomed, and a second shooter went down. Face-forward. One of the remaining two spun toward Z, and I shot him from behind the car. The last guy threw his gun on the street and turned and ran.

Z reached me.

"You want him?" Z said.

"You think you can catch him?" I said.

"The Cree named Z," he said. "All-American."

"Go," I said.

From a standing start, Z exploded down the alley. He'd been outrunning me in our interval training for several weeks. But this was like seeing some kind of different species. Z caught the shooter before he got to Arlington Street. He hit him in the back of the head with a forearm and the man went face-forward onto the ground. Z got hold of his collar and dragged him to his feet. And they came down the alley together more slowly than they'd gone up. I could hear sirens.

"Put the gun down on the ground," I said to Z. "Don't want the cops to shoot us while they are protecting and serving."

Without letting go of the collar of the guy he'd caught, Z put the .357 on the street. I put my .40 beside it. From Berkeley Street, a police cruiser came rolling through the barrels without even slowing; another came down the alley from Arlington Street, showing equal contempt for the barrels. Both cars stopped maybe ten feet short of us, and cops got out, shielding themselves with the open door, guns leveled at us.

"Put your weapons on the ground," one cop shouted. "Slowly."

I pointed at the guns on the ground.

"They're down," I said.

Two more cruisers showed up.

"Okay," the talking cop said. "Now you. On the ground, facedown, hands behind your heads."

Z frowned.

"Do it," I said.

We got down as instructed.

"You guys ever gonna forget the Little Big Horn?" Z said.

IT WAS LATE, and the crowd in my office had cleared. The stiffs in the alley had been taken away. The survivor had been hauled off, too, and only Quirk remained. We were having a drink.

"Sorry it took so long," Quirk said.

"Always does," I said.

"Coulda taken longer," Quirk said.

"I know that, too," I said.

Quirk nodded and rattled the ice around in his glass and sipped some scotch.

"Slug you didn't shoot is Warren Carmichael," he said. "We've known him for years. Says he was hired by one of the shooters, now deceased. Guy with a shotgun: Squirrel Rezendes.

Warren says he doesn't know why they were gonna hit you, or who hired Rezendes."

"And Rezendes, being dead, can't tell us more," I said.

"Yeah," Quirk said. "Nice going."

"Sorry," I said. "I was just trying to keep him from killing me."

"Sure," Quirk said. "It's always about you, isn't it."

"Who hired me in the first place?" I said.

"Price was right," Quirk said, and looked at Z.

"How about you," he said. "What do you get out of this?"

Z sipped his scotch.

"Squaw, two ponies," Z said.

Quirk looked at me.

"Who knew he was funny," Quirk said.

"Surprise to me," I said.

"Indians are always amusing," Z said.

"Sure," Quirk said. "What do you figure Jumbo's owners will do now that they've fanned twice."

"If at first you don't succeed," I said.

"Think they'll hire local talent again?" Quirk said.

"That hasn't worked out well for them," I said.

"They haven't hired wisely," Quirk said. "The business with the traffic barrels. Talk about overthinking something . . ."

"They'll send Stephano," Z said.

Quirk and I both looked at him. He sipped his scotch.

"Stephano DeLauria," I said.

"Alice's husband," Z said. "Nicky Fellscroft's enforcer."

"You know him?" I said.

"I've seen him," Z said. "And I've heard about him."

"I'm told he's good," I said.

"Hall of fame," Z said. "Like a man playing with boys."

"Like us," I said.

"Maybe better," Z said.

"I'll see what I can learn about Stephano," Quirk said.

"I'll make a call, too," I said.

Quirk nodded. He looked at Z again.

"Why are you so sure?" Quirk said.

"Been with Jumbo for a while. Pay attention. Everybody got a lot of faith in Stephano, and everybody scared of him."

"But you're willing to go up against him," Quirk said.

"Oh, sure," Z said. "Indians are always optimistic."

"And with so little reason," Quirk said.

"If you're right," I said to Z, "he may bring others."

"So did Custer," Z said.

"I DON'T THINK he's changed," Susan said. "You know him better than I do, but I think he has gotten rid of a lot of stuff that wasn't really Zebulon Sixkill."

"How'd he do that?" I said.

"He seems finally to have someone he can emulate," Susan said.

It was Sunday morning, and we were having a breakfast that extended into the afternoon.

"Me?" I said.

"You," Susan said.

She had drunk a small fruit smoothie, which had brought her past noon, and was now eating a single soft-boiled egg, with whole-wheat toast, which would probably take her to mid-afternoon.

"Well, who wouldn't emulate me?" I said.

"Everyone at Harvard," Susan said.

"Oh, them," I said.

"Z is, from my admittedly limited vantage, becoming more like you every day," Susan said. "Which suggests to me that he was probably a good deal like you to start with."

"Big and handsome, with a magnificent physique?" I said.

"Sure," Susan said. "It may be why he came to you in the first place."

"Because he was like me?"

"Because at some unconscious level, he may have sensed that he might be," Susan said.

"Think maybe that might be why I took him on?"

"Yes," Susan said.

"Seeing beyond the magnificent-physique similarities," I said.

Susan nodded.

"He did well at the shoot-out," she said.

"Just fine," I said.

She nodded.

"And so did you," she said.

"Good as ever," I said.

"In neither case was that because of how you looked," Susan said.

"Who you are is not always how you look?" I said.

"Not usually," Susan said.

"You look like a hot Jewess," I said.

"I'm the exception," she said.

"I'll say."

"Perhaps the booze and the broads and the bully-boy posture are all a kind of costume. If he learns what you know, and behaves as you behave, then it allows him to slough off the costume."

"So I haven't helped him change as much as I've helped him get out."

"Might be the case," Susan said.

"You Ph.D.'s," I said.

Susan smiled.

"We both spend our professional lives mucking around in the human condition," she said. "There is very little in there to be dogmatic about."

"I know," I said.

"Have a drink after the shooting?" Susan said.

"Quirk, Z, and I had two scotches each in my office, after everything was over with."

"He seem to want more?" Susan said.

"Hell," I said. "I wanted more."

"But you didn't have any," Susan said.

"No."

"I wonder if he did?"

"Did he go back to his room at Henry's gym and drag a bottle out from under the mattress?"

I shrugged.

"No way to know," I said.

Susan nodded.

"And if he did," I said, "nothing to be done."

"No," Susan said. "He has to do it himself, but if you matter enough, you may be able to help him simply by mattering. For what it's worth, I'm betting he didn't."

"I think he can do it," I said.

"Do you think he's right about Stephano Whatsisname?"

"Need to be ready for it, at least," I said.

"Have you talked with Mr. del Rio about him?" Susan said.

"I thought I'd do that tonight."

She stuck a piece of toast into her soft-boiled egg and bit off a corner.

"Good," Susan said.

"I KNOW OF NO ONE in Los Angeles who does not fear Stephano DeLauria," del Rio said on the phone when I finally got through.

He paused for a moment. I waited. The way he paused, I knew it wasn't my turn yet.

"Except Chollo," del Rio said. "To the best of what I know, Chollo isn't afraid of anything."

"If it gives him trouble, he assumes he can shoot it," I said.

"Exactly," del Rio said.

"And Bobby Horse?" I said.

"On his own," del Rio said, "yes, Bobby Horse would be cautious of Stephano. But with Chollo . . . He would go with Chollo into a working volcano."

"And you?" I said.

"I fear my wife," del Rio said. "Everything else Chollo and Bobby Horse take care of."

"So tell me about DeLauria," I said.

"He is an excellent hand fighter, a fine shot with handguns and long weapons. He is skilled with explosives. He is expert with a knife. Even a cudgel."

"Cudgel?" I said.

"I have worked very hard all my life to perfect my English," del Rio said.

"Lot of people have those skills," I said. "What makes Stephano especially fearsome?"

"His willingness," del Rio said. "He has been known, without malice, to kill a man, his wife, children, and dog."

"To make a point?" I said. "Or just because they were there?"

"Either," del Rio said.

"It doesn't bother him," I said.

"I believe he likes it," del Rio said.

"A skilled sadist," I said. "Who's found a profession suited to him."

"Yes," del Rio said. "Oddly, he seems devoted to his wife, and is thus entirely loyal to her father."

"Nicky Fellscroft," I said.

"Yes."

"Does he ever freelance?" I said.

"Stephano?" del Rio said. "No. He is Nicky Fellscroft's personal assassin."

"So if he went after somebody, it would be because Fellscroft told him to?"

"Or his wife told him," del Rio said.

"Fellscroft's daughter," I said.

"Yes," del Rio said. "And she would never point him at anyone without her father's agreement."

"Close family," I said.

"Very," del Rio said. "And one to which Stephano is very pleased to belong."

"It's worked out well for Stephano," I said.

"Do you expect him to come for you?" del Rio said.

"Possible," I said.

"Would you like me to have Chollo kill him for you?" del Rio said.

"You're very kind," I said. "But no, I need to deal with him myself."

"Yes," del Rio said. "You probably do."

IT WAS SUNDAY MORNING, in the full flower of early June. Susan and I were having brunch at a Boston restaurant called Mooo. The brunch was the stuff that dreams are made of, and so was Susan. I was sipping a passionfruit Bellini and having a very nice time when Tony Marcus slid into an empty chair next to me.

"Morning, Dr. Silverman," Tony said.

"Good morning, Mr. Marcus," Susan said.

"Call me Tony," he said.

"Call me Susan," she said.

He smiled. I checked the room. At a table for two a few tables removed was a young woman who looked like Halle

Berry. She smiled at us. Jittering at the bar was a skinny little youth named Ty-Bop who always looked like he was on something, and probably was. Whatever he was on didn't seem to impede him. He could shoot nearly as good as Chollo, or Vinnie Morris. Beside him was Junior, who was the approximate size of a 747 but organized differently. They were always in sight when Tony was around. At the other end of the bar, Z was drinking orange juice and eyeing Junior speculatively. Dueling bodyguards.

Junior saw me looking and nodded at me. Ty-Bop paid no attention. He never did, unless there was someone to be shot. When there wasn't, he seemed to spend his time contemplating the inside of his eyeballs.

"Nice brunch," Tony said.

"Elegant," I said.

"You try them Kobe beef dumplings?" Tony said.

"Soon," I said.

Susan was having assorted berries with champagne sabayon on the side, which had a fair chance of being more than enough for her. I had larger plans.

"We need a brief conversation," Tony said. "I was going to give you a call, but here we both are."

"Kismet," I said.

"Whatever the fuck that is," Tony said.

He looked at Susan, then at me.

"May I talk freely?" he said.

"When have you not?" I said.

"Not everyone likes to let the babe know everything," Tony said.

"I do," I said.

"Babe?" Susan said.

"You surely are a babe, Dr. Susan," Tony said.

"You're too kind," Susan said.

"Got cause to do some business in South Central L.A.," Tony said to me. "Some of the people I do business with do business with a fella named Nicky Fellscroft in L.A. You know who he is?"

"I do," I said.

"Got some interest in, ah . . ." He looked at Susan.

"In killing me," I said.

"Bingo," Tony said.

"Understand he already hire some local help, and they didn't work," Tony said.

"True," I said.

"My people in South Central ask me could I take care of that," Tony said.

"And you told them no, because you were too fond of me," I said.

"Tole them I drop you like a bad habit, you get in my way. But I don't do contract killing."

"See," I said to Susan.

"I make a lot of money. I don't need to hire out, you know?" Tony said. "Don't need the trouble. Don't need grief from the blue bellies."

"Thanks for the tip," I said.

"Ain't give it to you yet," Tony said. "Folks in South Central tell me he got his own man, fella named Stephano something. Say he'll probably send him. Say he badder than Hawk."

"They know Hawk?" I said.

"No."

"That's why they can say that," I said.

"I changed it a little," Tony said. "What they tell me was he the baddest mofo in the world. I sorta reworded it, cause of Dr. Susan. Course, they actually didn't say 'mofo.' "

"Did they say 'motherfucker'?" Susan asked sweetly.

"Matter of fact, they did," Tony said.

"Thought they might," Susan said.

"Other thing," Tony said, " 'fore I go back to my young lady and leave you folks in peace. You want me, I'll send some people over to watch your back. Can't give you Ty-Bop or Junior. They watch my back. But I got some pretty good folks I could, ah, dispatch."

"Thank you, Tony," I said. "But I need to take care of my own business, you know."

"I know," Tony said. "Knew it when I said it. But the offer is real."

He looked at Susan.

"You, too, Dr. Susan," he said. "Things don't go well, you need help, call me."

Tony took a card from his inside pocket and handed it to Susan.

"Thank you," Susan said. "That's very nice."

"He done me a favor once," Tony said. "I owe him."

"And," Susan said, "maybe your bark is worse than your bite."

Tony grinned at her.

"No," he said. "It ain't."

"YOU DIDN'T MENTION to me how fearsome Stephano Who-sis is supposed to be," Susan said.

"What good would that do you?" I said.

"None," Susan said.

"Besides," I said. "We both know how fearsome I am."

"I'll try to focus on that," Susan said.

Susan was still carefully ingesting her berries. Occasionally she would put a tiny speck of sabayon on one, and eat it.

"But you allowed Tony Marcus to speak of it in front of me," she said.

"I'm going to tell him that he can't speak freely in front of you?" I said.

Susan nodded.

"I might have found that bothersome," she said.

I ate a little tuna tartare.

"You know," I said. "I will withhold sometimes, when I think it's in your best interest."

She nodded.

"Yes," she said.

"But I won't conceal from you."

Again, she nodded.

"Yes," she repeated. "I understand the difference."

"Is it the Harvard Ph.D.?" I said.

"That's more of a work permit," Susan said. "Most of what I know, I've learned for my patients."

"How 'bout me?" I said.

Susan ate half a blackberry and smiled.

"You have been very helpful with my libidinous skills," she said.

"Glad to help," I said.

"Now that the cat is out of the bag," Susan said, "tell me about Stephano."

I told her what I knew. She listened the way she did, which is to say entirely. When I finished, she was nodding slowly.

"How fascinating," she said.

"Fascinating," I said.

"Everything in his life seems to reward his pathology," Susan said.

I was having some steak and eggs, trying to keep my cholesterol up. I ate some.

"Wife approves," I said. "Father-in-law/boss approves. Makes him a good living. He gets some variation on respect from his peers."

"Plus whatever pleasure he achieves by acting out his sadism," Susan said.

"Fulfilling," I said.

We were silent for a time. Susan ate a strawberry. I had some steak. At his table, Tony Marcus was leaning forward in deep contemplation of his brunch companion.

"You cannot," Susan said, "let him kill you."

"And leave you wrestling with your libidinous skills alone?" I said.

"I'd probably just abandon them," Susan said. "If you were gone."

"Be a great waste," I said, "of some highly developed technique."

Susan ate a blueberry. My left hand was resting on the table. She put her right hand on top of it for a moment.

"Well," she said. "Yes."

IT WAS LATE AFTERNOON. Z and I were sparring in Henry's boxing room, and Z was holding his own. We went five three-minute rounds. Z was still breathing comfortably when we stopped and went into Henry's office for beer.

Z held the cold bottle of Blue Moon against his forehead for a moment, then took a drink.

"Stuff I haven't told you," he said.

I drank some beer.

"Never too late," I said.

"I had a problem ratting anybody out," Z said.

I nodded.

"And I didn't trust you," Z said.

I nodded again, and drank some more beer.

"Figured maybe you were helping me out," Z said, "because you thought I knew stuff."

"Reasonable," I said.

"But you never asked me anything."

"It was a ploy," I said, "to gain your confidence."

Z looked at me silently for a moment.

Then he said, "No. It wasn't."

I shrugged.

"Never asked me about booze, either," he said.

"Figured that was up to you," I said.

He got two more beers from Henry's refrigerator and handed me one.

"You was a boozer," Z said. "And Susan said to you that she'd leave if you didn't give it up. . . . What would you do."

"Give it up," I said.

"I was you, I would, too," Z said.

We both drank some beer.

"But I got no Susan," Z said. "So I got to be able to stop on my own."

"Everybody does," I said. "Finally, it's just you."

"Just me," Z said.

"Yep."

"And you been working with me," Z said. "So I can be a guy who can win that one."

"According to Susan," I said, "I'm helping you be who you are."

"If you'd started pressing me for info," Z said, "we wouldn't have made no progress."

"I know," I said.

"Even now, I brought it up," Z said. "You aren't asking."

"No," I said. "I'm not."

Z held the beer bottle out a little away from him and studied it.

"When I finish this one, I'm gonna want another one," he said.

"Me too," I said.

"But I won't have one," Z said.

"Me either," I said.

The sun had slid considerably west by now, and the harbor water was much grayer than it had been when we came in.

"Jumbo and me are sitting in his hotel living room. We done a couple Violets, and we're drinking bourbon when the front desk calls and says there's a Ms. Lopata to see Mr. Nelson. I tell Jumbo. I tell him. He gives me a big thumbs-up, and I tell the desk to send her up. She comes in. She looks tense, you know? Jumbo gets some champagne, and they drink it and do some lines and she eases up. I stick with the bourbon. Coke gets me crazy sometimes. Always thought it didn't mix well with the muscle stuff I was juicing. After a couple lines, Jumbo says something slick, like, 'Come on into the bedroom, I got something to show you.' And he giggles—honest to God—giggles. And she looks down like she's gonna blush, but she doesn't, and they head on into the bedroom."

I sipped a small sip of beer. I was trying to nurse my second bottle so I could be a good example to Z.

"I'm nibbling at the bourbon and looking at the tube. I got

the sound up loud so I don't hear nothing, and they're in there maybe an hour. Then Jumbo comes out with no clothes on, which ain't pretty, and a really weird look on his face. And he says, 'Get in here, and help me.' And I go in and she's half on the bed, half on the floor, with this scarf around her neck, and the scarf's tied to the bedpost. She's naked, too . . . and Jumbo's saying, 'Get her on the bed, get rid of the scarf, get her clothes on, we gotta get her out of here.' And I say, 'What the hell happened.' And Jumbo says, 'Nothing, I didn't do nothing.' And I say, 'Is she dead?' And Jumbo says, 'I dunno. It's an accident.' And I get the scarf off her neck and try to listen to her heart and I can't find none. And I can't feel her breathing. And I say, 'I think she's dead.' And Jumbo says, 'We gotta get her outta here.' And I say, 'Shouldn't we get a doctor?' And he says, 'I don't know. I didn't do nothing. Get her dressed first. I don't feel good.' And he goes in the bathroom and starts to puke. And I get her up on the bed and put her clothes on her. You ever try to dress somebody like that? It is not easy. I gave up on the bra. Threw it away when I ditched the scarf. And Jumbo comes out of the bathroom, still no clothes on, and says, 'We gotta get her out of here.' And I say to him that the desk knows her name and knows she was here, and how we gonna get her outta here, anyway? And he shakes his head and goes out in the living room and drinks some of the bourbon out of the bottle and comes back in with his cell phone and says, 'I gotta call Alice,' and goes back in the bathroom and pukes again. Then he shuts the door. So I get her finished up, and now I'm pretty sure she's dead. And he comes out and says, 'Alice says when you got everything cleaned up, call the front desk and tell them a guest in your room is unresponsive. And then don't say anything to fucking anybody until she gets here.'"

Z finished the rest of his beer and put the empty bottle down on top of Henry's desk.

"So we tidy up, and Jumbo takes a shower and gets dressed. He tries to hide the scarf by putting it around his waist under his shirt, but he's too fat, so he has me do it around my waist. And he calls the front desk. You know the rest."

"Where's the scarf?" I said.

"After everybody left, I went out for a walk and put it and the bra in a trash can outside Quincy Market," Z said.

"Which they empty every night," I said.

"Long gone," Z said.

"Long," I said. "Jumbo ever tell you what happened?"

"Said she was drinking a lot of champagne. Says they was playing games with the scarf around her neck and he had to go to the bathroom, so he gets up and goes and closes the door. . . ."

"Always the gentleman," I said.

Z snorted.

"Yeah, he says while he was in the bathroom she musta passed out and rolled off the bed. He found her the way I said."

"You believe him?" I said.

"He was drunk," Z said. "She was drunk. Hell, I was drunk. Coulda happened. Or he coulda killed her. I got no idea."

"Only two people know," I said. "And one of them's dead."

JUMBO'S MOVIE WAS SHOOTING on a sunny day in the Rose Kennedy Greenway, where, not so long ago, the Central Artery had cast its shadow. The producer's name was Matthew Morrison. Z and I had coffee with him on the set, sitting in blue-backed director's chairs near the craft-services truck. There was a platter of turnovers on the counter.

"What kind of turnovers do you suppose those are?" I said.

"Usually some raspberry and some apple," Morrison said.

"Two of my faves," I said.

"What are the others?" Morrison said.

"Blueberry, strawberry, cherry, pineapple, peach, apricot, mince, blackberry, boysenberry . . ."

"Okay, okay," Morrison said. "I get it."

"Worst turnover I ever had was excellent," I said.

"Like sex," Morrison said.

"There's no such thing," I said, "as a bad turnover."

Morrison nodded. He looked at Z.

"Jumbo sees you on the set, Z," Morrison said, "he'll throw a shit fit."

"Eek!" Z said.

Morrison nodded.

"Seemed like I ought to mention it," he said.

"You know a man named Tom Lopata?" I said.

"It was his daughter . . . wasn't it?"

I nodded. A big guy wearing a cutoff Red Sox T-shirt and a tool belt bellied up to the craft-services counter and acquired some coffee and a turnover.

"You know him other than that?" I said.

"As a matter of fact," Morrison said, "I do. He was trying to sell us insurance."

"You personally, or the production?" I said.

"Insurance on Jumbo," Morrison said.

"Life insurance?" I said.

"Sort of," Morrison said. "With the production company as beneficiaries, in case Jumbo died or became disabled before he finished the film."

"Don't most movies have some kind of completion insurance?" I said.

"Of course," Morrison said. "But the poor dope didn't know squat about the business. He was just trying to sell insurance."

"What did you tell him?" I said.

"I explained to him that we had all that sort of thing in place," Morrison said.

"But let me guess," I said. "He didn't want to take no for an answer."

"He wanted to talk with Jumbo," Morrison said. "I told him that wasn't possible, that Jumbo didn't talk to people. He was pretty aggressive about it."

"Did he get to talk with Jumbo?"

"Oh, God, no," Morrison said.

"Maybe behind your back?"

Morrison shook his head. I noticed that there were still half a dozen turnovers on the craft-services counter.

"Jumbo's the franchise," Morrison said. "We keep a close eye on him. Ask Z."

Z nodded.

"I worked for Jumbo, but his manager paid me."

"Alice?" I said. "His agent?"

"Agent, manager, keeper," Z said. "All of the above. She paid the bill, and I was supposed to report anything out of the ordinary to the company and to her."

"But Jumbo could fire you," I said.

"Sure," Z said. "Jumbo got everything he wanted, as long as it didn't damage the franchise."

"Same deal with your, ah, successor?" I said.

Z shrugged and looked at Morrison.

"Same deal," Morrison said. "Jumbo can be self-destructive,

and we like to keep close tabs. Hell, I even followed up with Don, the new bodyguard. Lopata never got to Jumbo."

I looked at Z.

"Maybe Tom sent a messenger," I said.

Z nodded.

I shook hands with Morrison and thanked him for his time. Then I stood and went to the truck and took two turnovers.

As we walked away, Z said, "None for me, thanks."

"I didn't get any for you," I said.

And took my first bite.

STEPHANO DELAURIA CAME alone to introduce himself, on a drab June day with low clouds and rain spitting just enough to be unpleasant. I was at my desk and Z was standing with his arms folded on the top of the file cabinet, his chin resting on his forearms. He turned his head slightly to look at Stephano as he came into the office.

Stephano glanced briefly at Z. I opened the top right-hand drawer of my desk.

"No need for access to a piece," Stephano said. "I am not going to kill you today."

"Promises, promises," I said.

I left the drawer open.

"My name is Stephano DeLauria," he said. "Do you know who I am?"

"I do," I said.

Z hadn't moved. With his chin on his forearms, he looked steadily at Stephano. But there was about him a sense of potential kinesis, as if a spring was being coiled. Hawk was the only other person I'd ever known who gave off quite that kind of energy. Except that Hawk's spring was always coiled.

"Then you probably know why I've come to Boston," Stephano said.

His voice was very deep and flat. But it made the kind of throbbing purr that powerful engines make.

"I probably do," I said.

He smiled blankly, and we sat silently, looking at each other. His face was narrow. His features were sharp and prominent. His dark hair was combed straight back. He had a healthy outdoors look about him, as if he took long hikes.

"I have come to kill you," he said.

"Hot damn," I said.

He smiled again, a small, aimless smile, without meaning.

"It is my rule," he said. "I give one warning. If you stop what you're doing, I will go back to Los Angeles—disappointed, yes. But it is the way I do business."

"What is it I'm doing?" I said.

"We both know," Stephano said. "So does the Indian."

"And if I don't stop what we all know I'm doing?"

"It will give me pleasure," Stephano said. "It will allow me to kill you."

He looked at Z.

"Both of you," he said.

"Might be smart while it's two to one," Z said, "for us to kill you right now."

Stephano shook his head.

"I can kill you both now, if I must. Here, now, with your desk drawer open," he said. "But then it would be over quickly, and . . . I enjoy the process."

Z looked at me. I shook my head.

"So far it's all talk," I said. "Let's see what develops."

With his chin still on his forearms, and his gaze still fixed on Stephano, Z shrugged. Stephano stood.

"Down the road," he said, and walked out of the office.

I CALLED SUSAN.

"I am going to have to check out for a while," I said.

"Business?" Susan said.

"My appointment in Samara has arrived," I said. "I don't want to lead him to you."

She was silent for a little while.

Then she said, "Don't let him succeed."

"You know I wouldn't do that to you," I said.

"God, you're thoughtful," she said. "Can you stay in touch?"

"I can call," I said. "And I will."

"You sound like this will take a while," she said.

"I think so," I said. "I think he likes foreplay."

"So he *is* a sadist," Susan said.

"I would guess."

"While he's enjoying the foreplay, why don't you kill him?"

"I'm hoping to learn a little," I said.

"Besides which," Susan said, "you don't do that, do you."

"Only if it were about you," I said.

"You just plow along," Susan said. "You care about other people, but they don't dissuade you, or distract you."

"Except you," I said.

"Except me," Susan said. "You continue to be who and what you are, and you continue to do what you set out to do."

"Born to plow," I said.

"It scares the hell out of me," Susan said.

"Scares the hell out of me too," I said. "Sometimes."

"But I greatly admire it," she said.

"Good," I said.

"You might want to exploit his sadism in some way," Susan said.

"Suggestions?" I said.

"I don't have one," she said. "But if someone wants to stall for a while before he kills you, an opportunity might be lurking."

"Might at that," I said.

"Is Z with you?" Susan said.

"Yes," I said. "Though not at this moment."

"Where are you?"

"Home," I said. "With the door locked."

"At least you've locked the doors," she said.

"I always lock the doors," I said. "There's no advantage to not locking them."

"Always so logical," she said.

"Except when I'm not," I said.

"Except for then," Susan said.

We were quiet again. It wasn't awkward. Nothing was awkward with Susan. We both knew there was nothing left to say, but neither of us wanted to hang up.

"But Z will be staying with you when you are out and about," she said.

"He will," I said. "He'll come and walk me to my office in the morning. We'll probably have breakfast on the way."

"At the Taj?"

"Probably," I said.

"Don't overeat and get logy," she said.

I grinned silently.

"I'll be careful," I said.

"When do you suppose he'll have enough foreplay," Susan said.

"Same as everybody," I said. "When consummation becomes irresistible."

"I know the feeling," Susan said. "In a different context."

"Yes," I said.

"I hope to experience it soon again," she said.

"I'll do my very best to survive," I said.

"Call me when you can," she said.

After we hung up, I wandered to the front window and looked down at Marlborough Street. Stephano was there, under a streetlight, leaning against a car. There were three other men with him. Stephano was smoking. All of them were looking up at my apartment.

I opened the window and leaned out.

"Can you guys do harmony on 'Old Gang of Mine'?" I said.

They looked up at me silently.

"How about 'Danny Boy'? 'Won't You Come Home, Bill Bailey'?"

Silence.

"Want me to lead?" I said. "'Up a Lazy River'? You know that one?"

Nobody said anything; nobody moved except Stephano, who took a long drag on his cigarette and blew the smoke out slowly.

"Aw, you're no fun," I said, and closed the window.

I checked the lock on the front door, set the security alarm, and went to bed with a gun on my bedside table. There have been nights when I've slept better.

WHEN Z ARRIVED in the morning, I was showered and shaved and dressed for work. I had the little .38 in an ankle holster, and my new .40 S&W semiautomatic on my right hip. I still had the Browning nine-millimeter, but I kept it locked in the hall closet, as a spare.

Last night's quartet was no longer in front of my house, and we saw nothing of them as we walked to the Taj, but as we ate near the window on Newbury Street, Stephano stood outside and looked at us through the window. I smiled and shot him with my forefinger. He showed no reaction, and after a time, he walked away.

Z stared at the empty window for a time. Then he looked at me.

"You know," he said, "this is kind of fun."

"Except if we get killed," I said.

"But if we didn't run that risk," Z said, "what would be the fun?"

"Christ," I said. "A philosopher."

"Well, it's true. I mean, how exciting would this be if the winner got to capture the fucking flag? You know?"

"You played capture the flag?"

"Indian school," he said. "When I was little."

" 'Death is the mother of beauty,' " I said.

"What the hell does that mean?" Z said.

"Pretty much what you're talking about," I said. "It's from a poem."

"Oh," Z said. "That's why there's the part about beauty."

"You sure you weren't an English major at Cal Wesleyan?"

"Football," Z said. "What's that about death and beauty?"

"If there were no death, how valuable would life be?"

"Yeah," Z said. "Like supply and demand."

"It is," I said. "You got a weapon?"

"Got the .357," Z said. "And a bowie knife."

"A bowie knife," I said.

"I am a Cree Indian," he said. "The blood of Cree warriors runs in my veins."

"I'd forgotten that," I said. "You planning to scalp Stephano?"

"Get a chance and I'll cut his throat," Z said. "I'm good with a knife."

I nodded.

"Time to plow," I said.

"Plow?" Z said.

"Just an expression, I heard."

We finished our coffee. I paid the bill for breakfast and we left. There was no sign of Stephano and friends on Newbury Street. I looked at Z; he looked happy.

Maybe he's getting in touch with his warrior heritage.

I lowered my voice on the assumption that all warriors had deep voices.

"It is a good day to die," I said.

He glanced at me.

"For who?" he said.

"Old Indian saying."

"Paleface see-um too many movies," Z said.

I HAD a small idea.

It was late afternoon and raining hard when Z and I got in my car in the Public Alley behind my building, and pulled out onto Arlington Street. We circled the block and went down Berkeley Street to Storrow, into the tunnel under the city, southbound, and exited in time to cross Atlantic Ave and drive into South Boston. Stephano and his colleagues picked us up on Arlington Street and stayed close behind us, even bumping the rear of my car a little at the Boylston Street stoplight. I ignored them.

Jumbo's movie was shooting in the big alley between the Design Center and the Black Falcon Terminal in Southie. And when we parked near the set, Stephano and friends parked near us, and made a show of walking behind us onto the set.

So far, so good.

Jumbo was in his trailer, having lunch. Z and I went in without knocking. Don came to his feet, and put his hand inside his coat.

"Hey," he said. "You can't come in here."

"Can, too," I said.

I hit Don with a left hook and a right cross and knocked him over backward. It stunned him, and while he was recovering, Z bent over and took the gun from inside Don's coat and put it in the side pocket of his own raincoat.

"What the fuck is this," Jumbo said.

He was eating a sub sandwich and drinking champagne.

"Want to tell you some stuff, ask you some questions, and point something out," I said.

"What's that fucking Indian want?" Jumbo said.

He was trying to talk and eat his sub at the same time, and was making a mess of it. Don was sitting on the floor, recovering.

"Here's what I know," I said to Jumbo. "I know that Dawn Lopata was strangled to death on your bed, naked, with a scarf tied around her neck."

Jumbo looked at Z.

"The fucking Indian tell you that?" Jumbo said. "He's a lying sack of shit. Always has been."

"And that you had him dress her, and get rid of the scarf, before anyone called for help," I said.

"Fucking snitch," Jumbo said. "You think you can trust a fucking loser like Z?"

"Had you called for help right away," I said, "maybe she wouldn't have died."

"Bullshit," Jumbo said.

"And maybe you should go to jail for that," I said.

"Fuck you," Jumbo said, and drank some champagne.

"Good point," I said.

I walked to the window of the trailer. And leaned against the wall beside it.

I said, "How'd she die, Jumbo?"

"How the fuck do I know," he said, and stuffed more of his sandwich into his mouth. "I already told everybody what I know. I went to the bathroom, she was fine. I come out, and she was dead."

I nodded.

"You recognize Stephano DeLauria, if you saw him?" I said.

"Alice's husband," Jumbo said. "Yeah, a'course."

"That him?" I said, and nodded out the window.

Jumbo stared at me. Then he heaved himself up and came to the window. The rain blurred things a little. But Jumbo recognized Stephano.

"Jesus," he said.

Stephano and his posse were under an awning, leaning against the side of a Penske rental truck full of lighting gear. They were all four staring at Jumbo's trailer.

"Seem to be interested in you," I said to Jumbo.

Jumbo looked out the window at Stephano.

"What's he want?" Jumbo said.

"Maybe he's worried that if you get busted for the Dawn Lopata thing, you might start spilling your big gut about things involving Nicky Fellscroft and AABeau and all that," I said.

"I wouldn't say nothing about nothing," Jumbo said.

"You know that," I said. "And I know that. But does Stephano know that? Maybe more important, does Nicky Fellscroft know that?"

I stepped in front of the window and waved at Stephano. He extended his right arm, sighted down it, and pretended to shoot me with his first two fingers.

"Guess he's waiting until Z and I leave," I said.

"God, Jesus," Jumbo said.

His voice was shaking. He looked at Don, who was now sitting on the edge of the bed with his head in his hands.

"Fuck," Jumbo said. "Who's gonna help me?"

He looked at me.

"You," he said. "I'll give you as much as you want. You want the Indian, I'll hire him, too. Both of you. Say how much, you got it. Just keep Stephano away from me. Anything you want. Anything."

"The truth," I said. "You tell me what happened to Dawn Lopata, and maybe Z and I can help you out with Stephano."

"You know about him," Jumbo said. "What he does? What he's like?"

"I do," I said.

"I got nowhere else to go," Jumbo said. "You gotta help me."

"Tell me about Dawn," I said.

Jumbo took his champagne bottle from the ice bucket and drank about a third of it. He put the bottle down, belched hugely.

Then he said, "Fuck Dawn. These guys are gonna kill me, and you're worrying about some little slut from the fucking local boondocks?"

"Exactly," I said.

Jumbo guzzled some more champagne.

"I tell you what I know, you'll help me?"

"If I believe you," I said.

"How I gonna do that?" Jumbo said. "How can I make you believe me?"

"Can't," I said. "Gotta hope I do."

"That fucking sucks," Jumbo said.

"Does," I said. "Doesn't it."

Jumbo looked at his bodyguard.

"Lock the fucking door," Jumbo said. "Can you handle that?"

Don stood up and locked the door to the trailer.

"Useless fuck," Jumbo said.

"Hard to figure why you're having trouble finding help," I said.

OUTSIDE, THE RAIN was pounding. Inside the trailer, the plan was working better than I had ever hoped.

"Okay," Jumbo said. "I'm fucking her."

"Dawn," I said.

"Who the fuck else?" he said. "Little Bo Peep?"

"Or her sheep," Z murmured.

"Hey, man, you wanna hear or not?"

"Sure," Z said.

"I don't know what he tole you," Jumbo said to me. "But I'm speaking the God's-honest truth."

"Keep it up," I said.

"So we done pretty much everything I know how to do," Jumbo said, "which is a lot, and she wants me to try something new. So I'm game; she takes out this scarf from her purse, and ties it around the bedpost, then she loops it around her neck, but she keeps hold of one end, you know, so she can tighten it or loosen it. And then she tells me to do her again. That's what she said, 'Do me again.' So I'm game, and I do, and she tightens up the scarf and loosens it and tightens it, and it's like she passes out for a few seconds, and then loosens up and wakes up and, you know, really goes crazy. We been drinking some champagne and doing some dope most of the evening. I was kind of fucked up and starting to feel sick, so I tell her to hold on, and I go in the bathroom and . . . I'm sick for a while . . . and then I'm feeling better . . . and I clean up and come out, and she's hanging off the bed. She's got the scarf wrapped around her hand for some reason, and it didn't loosen."

"You think she passed out?" I said.

"Yeah," Jumbo said. "And—my luck—rolls off the bed and fucking chokes herself."

"Scarf was still around her wrist," Z said. "When I went in."

"And you had Z pretty everything up," I said.

Jumbo was looking out the window at the rain and the murky figures under the awning.

"Yeah, man," Jumbo said. "There is important money in this picture. I'm trying to save it, you know?"

"Heroic," I said.

"It's not my fault," Jumbo said.

"You know how she got to the hotel?" I said.

"Yeah," Jumbo said.

He continued to slug champagne from his bottle.

"Talk about a hoot, man," Jumbo said. "Her old man drove her in. He knew where she was coming, too. Even gave her a note to give me."

"The note say something about insurance?"

Jumbo raised his eyebrows.

"Yeah," he said. "It did. How you know all this shit?"

"I'm a trained investigator," I said.

"Whaddya gonna do about Stephano?" he said.

"Nothing yet," I said.

"But I told you the honest-to-God truth."

"Maybe," I said. "But the thing is, Stephano is not after you, at least at the moment. He's here to kill me."

Jumbo looked out the window again. There was nobody under the awning next to the truck. He looked back at me and started to speak, and stopped, and sat down suddenly.

He seemed smaller, as if he had imploded.

IT HAD GOTTEN DARK earlier than usual because of the clouds and the rain. We drove back from South Boston along Atlantic Ave in heavy traffic made heavier by the rain. Stephano and company had been parked next to us at the set, and were now behind us as we inched along.

"This is getting annoying," Z said. "Every time I see him, I think this is it. Is this when the balloon goes up?"

"The readiness is all," I said.

"Whatever," Z said. "It's working on me . . . which is why I suppose he's doing it."

"One reason," I said.

"There's another one?"

"It excites him," I said.

"And it gives him the chance to pick his spot," Z said.

"It does," I said. "But he won't act until the tension gets too big for him to hold off any longer."

"You mean like sex," Z said. "Foreplay, foreplay, then zoom."

"Something like that," I said.

We inched forward in the dense rush hour. The windshield wipers worked steadily. In the glistening rain, the traffic lights were jewel-like.

"Maybe we should pick our spot," I said.

"And hope he's ready?"

"If our spot looks really good to him," I said, "maybe he'll become ready."

Z nodded. I began to push against the traffic, deking and diving as if maybe I were in a panic.

"First thing," I said. "You want somebody to chase you, you gotta run."

Stephano stayed with us. In maybe forty minutes we pulled into a construction site, off Mystic Ave in Somerville, where a warehouse was being rehabbed into apartments. Most of the apartments would have a view of Somerville. Some expensive ones would offer the Mystic River.

We parked close, and made a dash through the rain into the building.

Even as our eyes adjusted, it was palpably dark inside. As we felt our way in, we encountered gutted-out lumber and tool stands, loose wires, sawhorses, and bales of insulation. Behind us, the doorless opening where we'd entered was a very slightly paler shade of black. There was a large obstacle in front of us, which felt like a pallet of bricks. We wedged around it and stopped and looked back at the faint opening where we'd entered.

"Now what?" Z said.

"We wait and see what develops," I said.

"Crees great warriors of the High Plains," Z said. "Crees mostly don't fight in warehouses."

"One might," I said.

"What if they don't follow us in?" Z said.

"Then the plan didn't work," I said.

"Then what?" Z said.

"We find another way to outwit them," I said.

THE FLOOR OF THE WAREHOUSE was concrete. There was no insulation in any of the exterior walls. The hard rain on the roof sounded through the whole building like a drum.

It took a half-hour, but the plan kicked in. There was just a hint of movement in the lesser darkness of the entrance.

"See that?" I murmured.

Z said, "Yes."

Then the electric purr of Stephano's voice cut through the blackness and the drumming of the rain.

"You can run, Spenser," he said. "But you can't hide."

"He thinks we're trying to hide?" Z said softly.

"Yes," I whispered.

"Isn't even a little afraid we might have set him up?" Z whispered.

"Too arrogant," I whispered. "And probably too eager. It's like he was dating us and we led him into the bedroom."

"And he's too hot to think," Z whispered.

"Be my guess," I whispered.

"Been there," Z whispered.

I smiled in the darkness.

"Most of us have," I whispered.

"You coming out of your hole, Tough Guy?" Stephano purred. "Or I gotta drag you out, squealing, by the tail."

"How come all the talk?" Z whispered.

"I had to guess," I whispered, "I'd guess he's attracting our attention while his people sneak around and try to find us."

"Maybe I'll sneak back at them," Z whispered. "Crees are great night fighters."

"I thought they didn't fight at night because if they were killed in the dark they wouldn't reach the happy hunting grounds?"

"What movie you see that in?" Z whispered.

"Can't remember," I whispered. "But Gene Autry was the star."

"He should know," Z whispered.

"I'll work left," I whispered. "You go right. We'll try to come in on each side of Stephano. Whichever of us gets there first kills him. And we'll try not to kill each other by mistake."

"Okay," Z whispered. "Then what?"

"Then we'll see," I whispered. "His pals may come for us, or they may run. Play it by ear."

"Think he'll stay where he is?"

"I think he'll keep talking," I whispered. "He wants to distract us, and I think he enjoys it, like all the rest."

"Come out, little rats," Stephano called. "Be men. Don't make us hunt you down like vermin."

"It is a good day to die," Z whispered, and left me.

The gutted interior of the warehouse was darkness visible. The litter of reconstruction made for very slow going. Particularly if you were trying to be quiet. I edged past something that felt like a sawhorse, and slipped under what felt like some loose wires. I stepped on a big timber with one foot and paused and felt around for a way past it. Probably a second-story floor joist. There were loose nails and screws underfoot. Enhanced by the wet weather, the black air was pungent with the effluvium of decay. I shuffled a few inches at a time. My gun in my right hand. My left forearm shielding my face.

Off to my right I heard a sudden scuffle of activity, sounding, in the thick silence, probably louder than it was. I stopped, listening. Again, silence. Was it Z, or was it one of Stephano's helpers? A wavering holler. *What the hell was that?* Then I figured it out. It was Z's version of a Cree war whoop. Z seemed to be rising to the challenge. There was no gunshot. The bowie knife must have proved useful. *One down.*

I smiled again. If I had been Stephano, the war whoop would

have creeped me out. It couldn't hurt. I inched along carefully, shuffle step by shuffle step, tediously edging around debris, containing the impulse to rush. I inched farther to my left, looking for the wall. Anything to give me some orientation. My shoulder hit something made of sheet metal. It rattled. I ducked low, and five rounds blasted past me as Stephano fired at the sound. I didn't fire back. He wouldn't be where he'd fired from. He wasn't that dumb.

I felt the wall with my left shoulder. With my shoulder against it, I felt along the wall toward where Stephano had fired. If it had been Stephano. I didn't bump into anything. Maybe the construction guys had cleared a passage along the wall. Stephano had no way to know if he'd hit me or not. Maybe I was dead. The uncertainty, coupled with the Cree war whoop, must have been stressful. Finally, sliding along the wall, I saw the faint square of lesser darkness, where we'd entered. I stopped. I couldn't really make out much in the way of shapes. I was looking for movement. What I got was a bonus.

"Spenser," Stephano said.

He was right in front of me.

"Let's stop fucking around with this," Stephano said. "You come to the door. I'll be there. We'll do it standing straight up, looking at each other, like two men."

I raised my gun and aimed toward the sound.

"I'm right here," I said.

And he moved. I fired at the motion, five shots as fast as I could shoot. I heard him grunt, and, after a moment, I heard him fall. I heard him breathe with a bubbly sound for a moment. Then I heard nothing.

I dropped to my hands and knees and crawled toward him. When I reached him, I put my hand out and felt him. I wasn't sure where I was feeling. But it didn't move. I felt around and realized I was on his leg. I traced up his leg to his stomach, then his chest, which was wet and warm. I found his throat and felt for a pulse. There was none. I stayed flat on the floor.

"Z," I said loudly. "I got Stephano."

From the darkness close by, Z said, "Yay."

"Two down," I said.

"Three," Z said.

"Wow," I said. "Quiet."

"Old Mr. Bowie," Z said.

I raised my voice.

"Okay," I said. "Last assassin. There's two of us, and you're alone. We've killed three of you already. I got no need to kill you, too. You sit tight, we'll leave, and you can go about your business. You do anything else, and we got all night. We'll find you and kill you."

Silence.

"Z," I said. "Can you see the door?"

"Sort of," he said.

"Okay, go for it and on out. Let me know it's you, as you come. I'll come out right behind you."

As he moved toward me through the blank darkness, heading for the hint of light that was the door, he began to sing softly.

"'Buffalo gals, won't you come out tonight, come out tonight, come out tonight?'"

Then I saw him move in the darkness as he went past me. On my hands and knees, I fell in behind him.

"'Buffalo gals, won't you come out tonight, and dance by the light of the moon?'"

I was pretty sure that the last assassin would take the offer. I holstered my gun, and felt the tension beginning to drain. As I followed Z through the open door, I found myself giggling at his song lyrics. In the rain we sprinted across the short open space to the car, and got in.

"Buffalo gals, won't you come out tonight?" I said, and started the car.

"Give white eyes a sense of Indian culture," Z said.

We pulled away.

"That's the best you could do?" I said.

"You knew it was me," Z said.

"That song has as much to do with Indian culture as Marshmallow Fluff," I said.

"Injun like'm Marshmallow Fluff," Z said.

IT WAS LATE. The rain was still raining. We sat at my kitchen counter with a siphon of soda, a bucket of ice, and a bottle of scotch.

I raised my glass toward Z.

"Pretty good," I said.

Z nodded.

"Ever kill anybody before?" I said.

"No."

We both drank some scotch.

"How you feel about it?" I said.

"Less than I thought I'd feel," he said.

"How you feel depends on stuff," I said.

"They would have killed me," he said.

"They would," I said. "And that helps with how you feel. Also, whether you knew them or not. If they died fast or slow. How close they were. What they looked like. It's easier at a distance."

"It was easier in the dark," Z said.

"Anything that distances you from the human fact of them," I said.

"Doesn't mean I liked it," Z said.

"Good," I said. "Stephano would have liked it. But it's worth remembering about yourself that you are the kind of guy who can stick a knife into someone in the dark."

"Are you like that?" Z said.

"Yes," I said.

"You wish you weren't?"

"No," I said. "But I keep it in mind."

"Why?"

"So I won't be that way when I don't have to be," I said.

Z nodded.

"You took Stephano out pretty nice," he said.

"I'm supposed to," I said.

"Yeah."

We didn't talk for a while. We finished our drinks at an easy pace, and made fresh ones. I could hear, faintly, the sound of the rain outside my front windows.

"Whaddya gonna do now?" Z said.

"I'm going to tell Quirk that I don't think Jumbo killed Dawn Lopata."

"You believe Jumbo?"

"Yes."

"Remember," Z said. "He's a lying fuck."

"Of course he is," I said. "But it's a plausible story, and nothing any of us knows contradicts it."

"Okay," Z said. "Then what?"

"Then Quirk does what he does," I said. "The DA does what he does. Jumbo's people do what they do."

"Can Quirk keep him out of jail?"

"Maybe," I said.

"What if he doesn't?" Z said. "What if they send him to jail?"

"I did what I could. I did what I said I'd do. That's all there is to do."

"Would it bother you?" Z said.

"Some," I said. "But I'd get over it."

"He probably should do time, anyway, for being a creep," Z said.

"Probably," I said. "Maybe he can make a deal."

"Swap Nicky Fellscroft for a light sentence?" Z said.

"Might," I said. "If they press charges."

"They might kill him," Z said.

"Also possible," I said.

"Easier than killing us," Z said.

I nodded. I could hear the rain outside my front windows. Z looked at his half-full glass.

"Ain't a lot of happy endings here," he said.

"There often aren't," I said.

"That's how it is," Z said. "Isn't it."

"'Fraid so," I said.

He nodded and sipped his drink and kept nodding slowly, as if in some kind of permanent affirmation.

"That's how it is," he said.

I don't think he was talking to me.

I SPENT THE MORNING with Quirk and a black woman
with wide-spaced eyes from the Suffolk County DA's office.
Her name was Angela Ruskin. I told them what I knew, and
what I thought. They listened.

When I got through, Quirk said, "I don't think there's
enough."

"We can't prove it didn't happen the way he said it did,"
Angela Ruskin said. "We might be able to get him for trying
to pretty up the scene."

"How much time would he do?" Quirk said.

Angela shrugged.

"Not much," she said. "Probably none, if Rita represents him."

"I don't want to arrest him," Quirk said.

"Because?" Angela said.

"Because I don't think he did anything. Unless being a creep is illegal."

"And you believe Spenser," she said.

"Yes," Quirk said.

She nodded and scanned the notes she had taken. Then she closed the notebook and stood up.

"I'm inclined to believe him, too," she said. "Despite all the publicity, this isn't a winner for us. We don't prosecute and we're giving him a bye because he's a big star. We prosecute and don't convict, it's because we're incompetent, and probably giving him a bye as well. We prosecute and convict and he's sentenced appropriately, we're all soft on him because he's a star."

"Only way to win is to get him convicted of something he didn't do, or get him a sentence that won't stand on appeal," Quirk said.

Angela smiled.

"I'll consult with my colleagues," she said.

After she left, Quirk leaned back in his chair with his hands clasped behind his head, and looked at me for a while.

"Heard there was three people killed at a construction site in Somerville last night," he said. "Two of them killed with a knife. One with a .40 caliber handgun."

"World's going to hell in a handbasket," I said.

Quirk nodded.

"Guy shot to death was Stephano DeLauria, who is the husband of Jumbo Nelson's agent."

"Tough on Alice," I said.

Quirk nodded.

"He was a button man," Quirk said. "For an L.A. Mob."

"Really?" I said.

"Had a big rep, I'm told," Quirk said.

"Well," I said. "I feel bad for Alice."

Quirk looked at me some more.

"I'll bet you do," he said.

I stood.

"We done?" I said.

Quirk nodded.

"Nice job," he said.

I said, "Thanks," and left.

I had one more thing I had to do.

TOM LOPATA'S OFFICE was in a converted storefront in Malden Square. There were several desks. Tom sat at the one closest to the door. The others were unoccupied.

He stood when I came in, and I could see him flipping through his mental Rolodex until he matched my face with a name. Then he stuck out his hand.

"Hey," he said. "Mr. Spenser, excellent to see you."

I didn't shake hands with him.

"I've stopped by to tell you what I know," I said. "I'm not telling anyone else. But I want to be sure that you know that I know."

"Sure," he said, and sat down. "Sure. I'll help you any way I can."

He gestured toward a chair. I stayed on my feet.

"You drove your daughter in to hook up with Jumbo Nelson," I said. "We know that. What only you and I know is that you did it because you hoped it would help you sell a big policy to him and the movie company."

"What are you saying?"

"I'm saying you pimped your daughter to a notorious pig. For money, and it got her killed."

"Why. . . What good does this kind of talk do now?" Lopata said.

"It doesn't do the kid any good. And I won't tell your wife or your son. I won't tell the cops. I won't tell anybody. But I want you to wake up every morning of every day and know what you did," I said. "Every morning."

"This is crazy," he said. "There's no way you could know this. I didn't do anything wrong."

I looked at him.

"I didn't," he said.

I didn't answer.

"I spent my life, for crissake, feeding them and buying them stuff I couldn't afford, and sending them to schools I couldn't afford. My fucking son is at Harvard. All I wanted was for her to put in a good word for me, just once. Is that fucking evil?"

"Yeah," I said. "In fact, it is."

"Come on," he said. "That's bullshit. I didn't do nothing so bad."

"Think about it," I said. "Every day."

I left.

WHEN I GOT BACK to Boston I changed into sweats, put some clean clothes and a shaving kit in a gym bag, and went down to the Harbor Health Club. I lifted weights. I hit the speed bag. I hit the heavy bag until the sweat was all over me and soaking through my shirt. Then I went to the steam room and sat for a long time. When I came out, I showered and shaved and put on my clean clothes.

It was still raining when I came out of the club. But it seemed to me that it was getting a little lighter in the west. Over Cambridge. Where Susan lived.

After the rain lifted, the world would probably seem as freshly washed as I was. The cleanliness was almost certainly illusory, or at best short-lasting. But life is mostly metaphor, anyway.

I got in my car and drove west.